Iain.

'What's the matter?' Pias asked as his wife sat bolt upright in bed.

'I can't tell you,' Yvette whispered, looking around. 'I don't know where they are. They could be anywhere, listening, watching. They'll kill me, they'll kill you if they knew I know. They can do it more easily than you can swat a buzzfly. Lady A was right, it will destroy the whole Empire.'

Pias had never seen Yvette this shaken. 'What can we do?'

Yvette's voice was determined as she said, 'We're getting the fastest ship we can and flying to Earth at top speed so I can warn the Head in person. And we're going to pray harder than we've ever prayed in our lives. First, we're going to pray that I'm totally, completely wrong. Second, if I'm not, we're going to pray that we're not too late to save at least some tatters of the Empire before it all collapses around us!'

By the same author

The *Lensman* Series

Triplanetary
First Lensman
Second Stage Lensmen
Grey Lensman
Galactic Patrol
Children of the Lens
Masters of the Vortex

The *Skylark* Series

The Skylark of Space
Skylark Three
Skylark of Valeron
Skylark DuQuesne

The *Family d'Alembert* Series (with Stephen Goldin)

The Imperial Stars
Stranglers' Moon
The Clockwork Traitor
The Bloodstar Conspiracy
Getaway World
The Purity Plot
Planet of Treachery
Eclipsing Binaries
The Omicron Invasion

Other Novels

Spacehounds of IPC
The Galaxy Primes
Subspace Explorers
Subspace Encounter

IMPRIMÉ EN FRANCE

E. E. 'DOC' SMITH
with STEPHEN GOLDIN

Revolt of the Galaxy

Volume 10 in *The Family d'Alembert* Series

GRAFTON BOOKS
A Division of the Collins Publishing Group

LONDON GLASGOW
TORONTO SYDNEY AUCKLAND

Grafton Books
A Division of the Collins Publishing Group
8 Grafton Street, London W1X 3LA

Published by Grafton Books 1985

Copyright © 1985 by Verna Smith Trestrail

ISBN 0-586-04343-8

Made and printed for
William Collins Sons & Co. Ltd, Glasgow

Set in Times

Dedicated to Ron Fortier—
a fan and a friend.

—S.G.

CHAPTER 1

A Stranger to DesPlaines

The heavy-gravity world of DesPlaines ranked reasonably high in galactic commerce. Sometimes called the "slagheap of the Universe," the planet was rich in heavy metals and precious stones, and did a creditable export business in those resources. The Circus of the Galaxy, owned and operated by the noble d'Alembert family, toured throughout the Empire and brought a sizeable amount of income into DesPlaines' coffers. Even the citizens themselves were a valuable commodity. With their lightning reflexes and above-normal strength, DesPlainians were always in demand as Marines, bodyguards, or criminals. By taking advantage of its geological and human resources, DesPlaines had turned a hellish environment into a prosperous and comfortable place for its natives to live.

One industry that was *not* big on DesPlaines, however, was tourism. People from worlds with more standard gravities—which included all but a tiny percentage of the settled galaxy—dared not visit DesPlaines without being surrounded by specialized equipment. The constant three-gee pull could easily provoke heart attacks and breathing difficulties even in people in superb physical condition. If that weren't bad enough, a simple fall—at three times the speed it would happen elsewhere —could prove fatal.

People from offworld usually dealt with DesPlainians via subetheric communications. If more personal contact was required, the DesPlainian often would visit the offworlder; sometimes a compromise would be reached and the offworlder would rendezvous with his DesPlainian contact on one of DesPlaines's three moons, where gravity was only one-fifth gee and everyone could relax. Only the most desperate circumstances could compel someone from a normal-grav world to visit the surface of DesPlaines itself.

There were other high-grav worlds, of course, the most well-known being Purity and Newforest, but their citizens seldom traveled. The Puritans shunned the spiritual contamination they felt would be inevitable if they had much intercourse with people less wholesome than themselves. The Newforesters were a clannish group who preferred their own sometimes backward ways, and who had until recently kept apart from the mainstream of galactic society.

Thus the major spaceports on DesPlaines were designed primarily with cargo in mind. There were some passengers, of course; with DesPlainians in such demand throughout the Empire there were always some departing for or returning from other worlds. But DesPlainian spaceports tended to be large, open, barnlike buildings with plain walls and few of the amenities to be found in more well-traveled ports. The walls were not hung with colorful displays of DesPlainian night spots or scenic wonders; the few chairs scattered about the floor were institutional and uncomfortable. The faded tile on the floors was clean but badly scuffed; there was little point in improving it when so few people ever saw it in the first place. The harsh lighting cast sharp shadows on the walls and floors, and the air perpetually smelled of perfumed disinfectants.

2

Today, though, the freighter *Anatolia* brought with it a paying passenger whose destination was indeed Des-Plaines. She was a young woman, perhaps twenty years old, with long black hair and a deep olive complexion. She had enormous brown eyes and thick, sensuous lips that highlighted her attractive face, and she wore a bright-colored blouse and a skirt with a wild, multi-colored pattern.

Even under normal circumstances she'd have attracted every masculine eye in the spaceport, but her bearing showed nervousness and not a little apprehension. Something was not quite right with her, and that made her stand out even more.

Her nervousness brought her to the attention of the SOTE clerk checking identification. One of the many duties of the Service of the Empire was to keep records of the comings and goings of the Empire's citizens, and to serve as customs agents to prevent the transport of contraband materials. Spaceport clerks were trained to spot suspicious behavior—and this traveler was definitely exhibiting some.

Courtesy was ever the watchword of the Service of the Empire—when more drastic measures were not called for. "Good afternoon, gospozha," the clerk said politely. "May I see your ID card, please?"

The woman fumbled awkwardly in the compart-mented leather belt she wore and eventually produced the card. The officer took it and inserted it in the scanner, which immediately read the encoded information and informed him that the card was issued to "Beti Bavol," that she held the title "lady," and that her physical description matched that of the woman standing before him. She was from the planet Newforest and consequently could be expected to have the typical high-grav physique: short, well-balanced body with thick bones and toughened muscles. That much, at least, checked out.

"May I ask Your Ladyship to look in the retinascope for a positive ID scan?" the clerk continued. The fact

3

that Gospozha Bavol was of the nobility meant that even more courtesy was called for, but he was still suspicious.

Beti Bavol peered into the scope, and a quick comparison with the patterns on her ID card confirmed that she was indeed who she claimed to be. At the same time, the clerk surreptitiously had the desk's built-in scanner go over her luggage and clothing to see whether she was carrying anything illegal. The scanner showed she had a small knife tucked under her clothing next to her hip, but nothing more serious than that. There was nothing illegal about carrying a hidden knife—many women did it for protection—but it was one more factor to be considered.

"Thank you," the officer said as Beti Bavol pulled her eyes away from the scope. "Are you visiting Des-Plaines for business or pleasure?"

"I . . . I'm not sure. That is, I'm looking for someone, my brother. I think he may be here. I guess you'd call that pleasure."

The clerk did not respond; he was busy trying to make a decision. He had the full authority to arrest this newcomer just on the basis of his feeling that something was wrong, but authority that powerful could not be wielded casually—especially not against a member of the nobility—and he had no hard evidence to back up his suspicions. At the same time, he didn't feel completely right about letting her go off unsupervised.

In the end, he made a compromise decision. He entered her card number into his computer with the order to keep a check on her activities and look for anything further out of order. Whenever her ladyship took a hotel room, rented transportation, ordered a meal, or made any major purchase, the fact would be reported to SOTE. The Service could then decide on the basis of more information what action should be taken.

Ejecting the ID card from the machine, the officer handed it back to the young woman from Newforest. "Thank you for your cooperation, Your Ladyship," he said politely. "Enjoy your stay on DesPlaines. Good luck in finding your brother."

Because there were so few tourists, there were no hotels near the spaceport; Beti Bavol had to take a cab into the center of Nouveau Calais to find one. The price was reasonable, and she quickly settled into her comfortable but compact room. She unpacked her one small suitcase and then faced the challenge of what to do next.

It was imperative that she find her brother Pias as quickly as possible—but where could she begin? She didn't have enough money with her to hire a detective, and she'd never done any tracing on her own, so she hadn't the faintest idea how to go about it. She had very few facts to go on. Her brother had been exiled from Newforest four years ago in disgrace and she wasn't even sure he'd come to DesPlaines. All she knew was that he'd become engaged to a DesPlainian woman named Yvette Dupres. They could just as easily have married and settled on some other planet—or perhaps they'd broken their engagement and each gone their separate ways. It was a very slender thread that brought Beti Bavol to DesPlaines—and if it broke, she wasn't sure where she'd go from here.

She tried calling the police first, but they were less than helpful. Unless her brother was officially listed as a missing person or was wanted in connection with some crime, they couldn't spare the manpower to help her. Since Pias's case didn't fall within the "missing persons" category, the police refused even to listen to her.

She next tried calling the SOTE office, figuring that they would have records of everyone who came to DesPlaines. The clerk she spoke to told her that they might indeed have such records, but they were all confidential; regulations regarding personal privacy forbade SOTE to release such information to the public without a court order. Beti Bavol had hit another stone wall.

She checked the public vidicom directory; if Pias had

5

a vidicom set, he'd more than likely be listed. But there was no listing for anyone with the name Bavol. There were plenty of Dupres', including seven Yvettes; in desperation Beti called them all. Three of them weren't in; the rest were obviously not the woman she'd met as Pias's fiancée.

Wracking her brain, Beti tried asking information from the Bureau of Public Records. If Pias and his Yvette had gotten married, there should be a certificate on file somewhere. A very kindly lady checked the entire file for her, but could find no marriage certificate issued to Pias Bavol. If Beti's brother had gotten married, the ceremony had taken place somewhere other than DesPlaines.

By the time she'd received this negative information it was suppertime and most government offices had closed for the day; there would be nothing Beti could do until they opened again tomorrow. Feeling miserable and depressed, she went to dinner at the small restaurant adjacent to the hotel. There, as she picked apathetically at her food, she tried to think of some other strategy for finding Pias.

Perhaps she could check with the transportation department and find out whether Pias had ever applied for a license to drive or fly a vehicle on DesPlaines. Perhaps she could check to see whether any business licenses had been granted in his name. And—though the thought horrified her—she supposed she should check the newsroll obituaries over the last few years to see whether he might have died here.

She considered taking out a personal ad in the local newsrolls, but discarded that thought as impractical. She couldn't even be certain he was on this planet—and even if he was, the odds were greatly against his seeing the ad. Her funds were running very low after paying for passage on the *Anatolia*; she dared not waste her money on anything that offered such small chance of success.

She returned to her room and tried to get involved with the programs on the trivision and sensable, but she

6

simply couldn't concentrate. She'd pinned so many of her hopes on locating Pias quickly, and now she was feeling lost and helpless on a strange world, without friends or family to give her the support and encouragement she needed to carry on. She stared listlessly at the images in the trivision cabinet, then switched it off in frustration. Donning the nightgown she'd brought with her, she went to bed and, after tossing and turning for over an hour, finally fell asleep.

If she hadn't been so nervous, her story might have ended there. But, edgy as she was, she awoke in the middle of the night to the strong feeling of danger and the certain knowledge that something was horribly wrong. Her heart fluttered in an irregular rhythm as she tried to bring her mind fully awake so she could focus on the problem.

The room was almost pitch black; the heavy curtains cut out all but a fraction of the street lights outside the hotel. There was no smell of smoke, so it wasn't the threat of a fire that had awakened her. She strained her eyes against the darkness and, at the same time, held her breath so she wouldn't miss the slightest sound that might alert her to the trouble.

There it was, a faint scratching noise at the door. Someone was working quietly on the lock, trying to break into her room. With that realization came the certain knowledge that this was not some ordinary hotel sneak thief. This could only be someone hired by her brother Tas to bring her back to Newforest before she could talk to Pias—or to kill her.

Her first impulse was to grab the com unit beside the bed and call hotel security, but then she heard the faint click of the lock opening. She could be very, very dead before security managed to send someone up here.

She reached under her pillow and grabbed the hilt of her knife, kept there for just such emergencies. Then, pushing the bedcovers aside, she slid silently across the room to take up a position behind the opening door. The intruder was moving slowly and carefully, trying not to make any sound that would alarm his victim.

This gave Beti time to brace herself for the action that was to come.

The few seconds that she stood there in the dark stretched out immeasurably, and her heart was pounding so violently in her chest she was sure it would alert the intruder to her presence. Her hand trembled slightly. She held the knife point upward as she'd been trained to do, and was grateful that it was considered necessary for everyone in the Gypsy culture of Newforest to learn how to fight with a knife, even female members of the nobility.

As the door opened slowly, a ribbon of light streamed in from the hall outside. At first Beti could see nothing from her position, but she heard the unmistakable hum of a stun-gun and supposed her would-be attacker had fired at the tangle of covers on the bed, thinking she was asleep there. Then, perhaps feeling a little more confident, the intruder opened the door wider and stepped inside the room.

Beti forced herself to wait until she had a clear view of him before she acted. Then, taking two quick steps forward, she brought her knife up hard under the man's ribs. For all her practice at knife fighting, this was the first time she had actually stabbed anyone, and it was a jolt to feel the impact of her knife digging through living flesh. She had no time, though, to be shocked by what she'd done. Her only thought was to kill, or at least incapacitate, this man who'd meant to do her harm.

The man gave a gasp of surprise and pain as the blow hit, and turned awkwardly to look at his assailant. He tried to shift position and shoot her but the shock of the stab wound was too much. The gun dropped from his hand and he crumpled to the floor, nearly taking Beti's knife with him. Only her nervously tight grip on the handle enabled her to pull the blade out as the man fell.

A hand grabbed her shoulder from behind, and Beti realized with horror that the intruder had not been alone. She whirled and slashed the man who'd grabbed her. A line of blood appeared across his forehead and he yelled with pain, letting go of her. But Beti could see the silhouette of a third man behind him, and her heart fell as she realized she would have a very difficult time escaping from this trap.

She pushed hard at her second attacker, knocking him against the doorframe. Sidestepping him and crossing the threshold, she approached the third man and swung her knife at him. The blade didn't come near him, but he backed away, seeing what she'd done to his companions. His small retreat gave her enough of an opening to run past him and down the hallway. Beti raced down the carpeted corridor, yelling for help at the top of her lungs. She didn't really expect anyone to open their doors, but maybe someone in one of the rooms would call security—if only to complain about the shrieking madwoman who was ruining their sleep.

The third man must have been the most heavily armed, because a blaster bolt sizzled the air and missed the fleeing woman by just a few centimeters. The second man hissed, "Not in here, you fool," and the blasterfire stopped, but that one shot had lent great speed to Beti's feet. As the two men started in pursuit, Beti turned a corner in the hallway and started looking for a way out.

At the end of this hallway was a door marked as a fire exit. On high-grav worlds like DesPlaines, buildings were seldom more than two stories tall and this hotel was no exception. Beti's room was on the second floor, with a series of stairs serving as an emergency route to the ground. Beti practically flew through the door, but went down the stairs cautiously. Natives of a high-grav planet learned to deal carefully with any changes in elevation; even a short fall could mean broken bones at the least, possibly even death. Beti did not want to let her assailants accomplish their mission by default.

The would-be killers came through the second-floor door just as Beti reached ground level. The one with the blaster shot again. His beam burned into the exit door just as Beti was reaching for it. She barely hesitated. Yanking the door open, she raced outside into the cool night air.

Beti found herself in a darkened alley that ran alongside the hotel. The ground was cold and damp against her bare feet. She paused for an instant to get her bearings. The main street lay to her left, about thirty meters away. Taking a deep breath, she ran toward the street and bumped into a stack of boxes that was standing in the darkness at the side of the alley. She cursed at the pain as she bruised herself, then began running once more for the street. Her feet made a light padding sound as she ran, a counterpoint to her harsh gasps for breath.

The two men were still chasing her. Apparently unwilling to risk blasterfire in public, they probably hoped to wear her down and catch her before she could reach some place of safety.

At this hour of the night there was no one else on the street, and little motorized traffic. Even the front door to the hotel was security-locked by now; Beti would have to stop at the door and identify herself to the clerk on duty before she'd be let in, and she dared not pause that long for fear her pursuers would catch up with her.

Beti was running short of breath; her gasps grew louder and longer. Sensing this, the two men behind her quickened their pace. They were stronger and faster than she was and were not running in bare feet; they were confident they could catch her before much longer.

A car zoomed by on the darkened street. Beti stood in front of it waving her arms, trying to flag it down, but the driver refused to stop. Beti had to jump out of his way to avoid being run down, and then resumed her flight. She could tell her pursuers were gaining on her, but she couldn't move any faster. Newforest's gravity was two-and-a-half gees; DesPlaines' measured closer to three. The difference was slight, but under such trying circumstances it was significant. With each step she took, Beti wore herself down further as she fought the slightly higher gravity.

Beti ducked into another alleyway, hoping to escape through it onto some other street or at least find someplace to hide. She ran down the darkened alley. Each breath was a fresh stabbing pain in her lungs.

Too late she realized she'd come to a dead end. She

found herself facing a brick wall, with no way to climb over it. She looked from side to side for an open doorway, but there was none. It was too late to go back the way she'd come. She was trapped. Even as her spirits were sinking, she turned back to face her pursuers, knife at the ready. If her life was to end in some dead-end alley on a planet far from home, at least she would end it with a fight.

The two men chasing her had slowed their pace, realizing they had her trapped. The man with the blaster was still reluctant to use it, but they approached slowly out of respect for her talents with the knife. Beti stood in a fighting crouch, waiting for them to come within range so she could at least kill one before the other overpowered her.

Suddenly bright lights appeared at the front of the alley and a loudspeaker blared, "This is the police. Drop your weapons immediately and put your hands in the air."

The two men whirled around at this unexpected development, and the one with the blaster pointed it at the lights. He never had the chance to fire as the buzz of a stunner charged the air and he collapsed in a heap on the ground. His partner, realizing they'd lost, surrendered to the inevitable and put up his hands.

Beti flushed with sudden relief and she staggered, then leaned against the wall for support. She let the knife drop to the ground. She wouldn't need it. Her ordeal was over for the moment—and maybe now she could convince the police to help her look for her brother.

CHAPTER 2

A Family Reunion

Felicité, the mansion of DesPlaines' Duke Etienne d'Alembert, was a sprawling one-story complex surrounded by sturdy stone walls. The maze of hallways connecting the thirty major rooms and the hundred and ten bedrooms had been known to confuse even the sharpest minds—so much so that small computer terminals were located at intervals to calculate and pinpoint the shortest route from wherever one was at the moment to wherever one wanted to go.

This enormous edifice was usually barely occupied, as Duke Etienne and the majority of the d'Alembert clan toured the Empire in the Circus of the Galaxy for no less than ten months out of the year. In those months the estate was inhabited by Duke Etienne's eldest son Robert, Marquis of DesPlaines, Robert's wife Gabrielle, their three children, and the host of servants and administrators it took to run both the household and the planet. Only when the Circus was on vacation was Felicité crowded to capacity, and then even the barracks behind the main mansion would be filled with d'Alemberts practicing new tricks and upgrading their acts.

The Circus was currently on tour, but nonetheless there were a few extra residents at Felicité. Yvonne d'Alembert and Pias Bavol were between assignments for the Service of the Empire and had nothing more crucial to do than tend their children, Maurice d'Alembert and Kari Bavol.

The d'Alembert family tradition was a rigorous one, and already the children were being taught the skills they'd use in later life. At one year of age, Maurice was learning the art of tumbling and how to fall properly—important lessons for anyone from a three-gee world, and particularly important for someone who would probably end up in the Galaxy's foremost circus troupe. Yvonne also took her son for swings on a trapeze to help him overcome the fear of heights instinctive to every high-grav native. Yvonne d'Alembert had married into the circus clan and was not a performer herself, but she was a skilled athlete and could follow the strict Circus regimen for child training.

Kari Bavol, six months old, was still a bit young for such vigorous activities, but her father took her into the swimming pool every day and taught her enough swimming to "drownproof" her while she learned not to be afraid of the water. Pias, though in superb shape, was neither a performer nor an athlete, and while he loved his daughter, he looked forward to the day when he could hand her over to some of the Circus's more skilled teachers, who'd give her a more complete education than he could ever hope to impart. In the meantime he did the best he could, and any skills he lacked as an instructor were more than compensated for by fatherly affection.

The days were spent quietly in childrearing, reading, and casual conversation, but the peace was deceptive. While Pias and Yvonne projected an image of cool serenity, both were torn with worry over the fate of their spouses. Yvonne's husband Jules and Pias's wife

Yvette were currently on assignment for SOTE—an assignment that could be the most dangerous of their careers as secret agents. Jules and Yvette had gone to the planet Omicron in company with the Galaxy's most nefarious traitor, Lady A, to investigate the possibility that the Empire was under attack from a hostile alien force. Pias and Vonnie had been unable to accompany their mates, and could only stay home and worry about what might be happening to them. Both knew they would have trouble sleeping until they knew the fate of their beloved partners.

Several days after Jules and Yvette had left for Omicron, Felicité received a midmorning vidicom call from Baron Ebert Roumenier of Nouveau Calais, Vonnie's father. After inquiring about the health of his daughter and his precious grandson, the baron got down to business. "Actually," he told Vonnie, "I'm calling to speak to your brother-in-law Pias. Does he have a sister named Beti?"

When Pias was brought to the vidiphone and the question was asked, he sat upright and his body tensed. "What's happened?" he asked. "Is she there? Is everything smooth?"

"She had a bit of a fright last night, but she's recovered," Ebert said, and went on to recount the police version of what had happened. "She refused to say why the men tried to kill her, and the men only know they were hired to do a job. Lady Bavol said she refused to discuss the matter with anyone except her lost brother Pias, whom she thought might be on DesPlaines. Since she's a member of the nobility the police brought the matter to my attenion, and I've invited her to stay here as my guest until the business is settled. I thought I'd contact you so we could figure out what to do."

"Thank you," Pias said. "I'll be over there as fast as I can. Tell her I'm coming, but don't give her any details about . . . well, about my business or the family I've married into."

The baron nodded. His family was also involved with the Service, and he knew the value of keeping secrets.

Yvonne offered to come with Pias, since she hadn't visited her father in several weeks. The two agents and their children climbed into the personal copter and started the ninety-minute flight to Nouveau Calais.

Not much was said during the trip. As Vonnie looked across at Pias she could see conflicting emotions playing across his features. In all the years Vonnie had known him, she'd never heard Pias say a single word about his family—but she'd gotten enough of the story from Yvette to understand some of the pain behind his silence.

When Pias and Yvette were engaged, Pias took his fiancée to Newforest to meet his family. There he learned that his father had contracted an incurable disease and that his younger brother was plotting against him. Because of the secret nature of his job, Pias couldn't tell his family the real reason why he couldn't stay on Newforest, and his brother used that as a weapon against him. Accusing Pias of abandoning his family and the traditional Gypsy lifestyle, the brother had a council of elders—with Pias's father, the Duke of Newforest, sitting in judgment—declare Pias a nonperson. He was cast out of the family and no one on the planet would have anything to do with him. Pias Bavol, who should have had the title of marquis and should have become Duke of Newforest at his father's death, had been wiped from his people's minds as though he'd never existed.

More than once during the last few years, when the planet Newforest was mentioned, Vonnie had seen Pias go cold and quiet. She'd tried to imagine what it would be like to have her entire family and every childhood acquaintance suddenly ignore her very existence, to have shopkeepers turn away from her when she tried to order something, to suddenly become a phantom in the world of the living. The pain would be more than she could bear, and she'd always marveled at Pias's strength to shoulder such a weighty burden in order to stay with the woman he loved.

Somehow, with the love and support of his new fam-

15

ily and his job as a secret agent of the Service, he'd built a new life for himself that hardly ever touched on the old one he'd lost. And now, without warning, into that new life came a painful reminder of all he'd left behind: a sister, obviously in some kind of trouble, needing his help after scorning him all these years. That had to be a nasty shock—yet, knowing Pias as she did, Yvonne was sure he wouldn't turn his back on such a plea.

Vonnie tried hard to recall what Yvette had told her about Pias's family, and particularly about his sister Beti. There wasn't much, just that Beti had been a teenager when Yvette met her and seemed pleasant enough at their one encounter, before Pias was ostracized. It was not enough material on which to form an opinion; Vonnie would have to wait until they arrived at her father's house and the situation was more fully explained.

The Roumenier baronial estate was in the middle of a small park in the northeast quarter of Nouveau Calais. Pias landed their copter on the heliport roof and Vonnie led him and the children down the familiar stairs into the home where she'd grown up. A servant told them the baron and his guest were awaiting them in the drawing room.

Beti Bavol looked up the instant they walked into the room, and an electric current passed through the air between brother and sister. Vonnie noticed that Beti was a very pretty girl, and the resemblance to Pias was unmistakable.

The silence seemed to drag on forever, until Pias finally broke it. "Hello, Beti," he said. His voice was quiet, subdued, as though he were speaking from a great distance.

"Pias, I . . ." Beti hesitated, then rethought what she'd been about to say. "You're looking well," she said formally.

"You look so different I'd hardly recognize you," Pias told her. "So grown up. Of course, it's been years. . . ." He realized he was touching on a delicate

16

subject and his voice trailed off indecisively. Trying to fill the conversational gap, he added, "This is my sister-in-law, Yvonne, and her son Maurice. And . . . and look, Yvette and I have produced a niece for you, little Kari."

Beti's eyes went wide, and for the first time the tension in her face began to ease. "Oh Pias, she's darling. Come, let me hold her."

As Pias brought the child over to his sister, Beti continued, "Where is Yvette? Is she well? Are you and she still together?"

"She's away on business right now," Pias said carefully. "I'm sure she'd be glad to see you again if she were here."

Baron Ebert Roumenier cleared his throat. He was shrewd enough to know when his presence was not required. "Yvonne, why don't you and I take Maurice for a walk through the garden? Really, you don't bring him over for a visit nearly often enough." Father, daughter, and grandson departed tactfully, leaving the room to the Bavols.

Silence descended on the room again. Beti Bavol held her little niece on her lap and refused to meet her brother's gaze. It was left to Pias to break the silence once more.

"They tell me you're in some kind of trouble," he said as he sat down next to her on the couch, "that there are some people trying to kill you. What's the matter? What's wrong?"

Beti looked suddenly into his face, and there were tears in the corners of her eyes. "Oh Pias, I've done you such a terrible wrong. We all have. There's no way I can ever say I'm sorry for all the hurt. I didn't want to do it; I always liked you. But I was only a girl, I couldn't fight them, I didn't know how to try. It was safer just to go along with the rest, to pretend you weren't there. I've thought about you a lot in the past years, wondering where you were and what you were doing. But I could never say anything out loud. . . ." Her sobbing became

17

too great for her to continue. Throwing her arms around her brother's shoulders, she wept, unashamed.

Pias held her gently and didn't try to speak. He had his own eyes closed, trying to purge himself of the bitterness and pain he felt. Beti wasn't to blame for what had happened to him; as she'd said, she was only a teenager when the *kriss* voted to oust him from Newforest society. A young girl could do nothing against such overwhelming social pressure. His true complaint, he knew, was against other people, older and more in control of worldly affairs. A large part of him wanted to tell Beti to go away and not reopen an old wound that had almost healed by now—but a larger part of his heart and conscience told him he could not turn her away when she was in so much trouble.

When her sobbing finally subsided, Pias asked her, "Has the *kriss* revoked its decree?"

Beti shook her head sadly. "Not with Tas running it. They wouldn't dare."

"Poppa's still duke, isn't he?" Despite his avowed disinterest, Pias kept watching the newsrolls for items about Newforest. He'd seen no mention of his father's death—but he was often away on assignment, and Newforest was a rather unimportant planet. A change in administrations would not be major news elsewhere in the Galaxy.

"He's hanging on," Beti said, sniffing back the last traces of tears. Though mottle fever was incurable, it was a lingering disease that could drag on for many years before killing its victim. "You know how tough he is."

"But Tas is running the *kriss*," Pias reiterated.

"Tas is running *everything*," Beti said. "According to the edict, he's now the oldest child, due to become duke when Poppa . . . goes. Poppa gets weaker and weaker, and it's all he can do to stay alive. He doesn't have the strength to fight Tas, too. Tas acts like he's already duke—almost like he's emperor. If you think I'm hard to recognize, you ought to see him. He's a dictator, telling everyone what to do and think. Anyone

18

who stands up to him gets beaten, sometimes even killed."

"Has a report been filed with the Service of the Empire? I know the Empress takes a dim view of subordinates who get too far out of line. She wouldn't tolerate such behavior if she knew about it."

Beti shook her head. "Nobody dares file a report. Tas seems to know everything that's going on everywhere on the planet. I don't know how he does it, he can't have that many spies, but he just *knows*—and he makes things very rough for people who oppose him."

Pulling her head back slightly she gazed straight into Pias's eyes. "What went wrong with him? I don't understand. You and he were always my big brothers, people I could run to when I was hurt. Tas was always full of life, always wanting to play new games with me. He was never like this, never cruel. It's as though something in him, whatever it was that made him human, just turned off suddenly."

"I know he was always jealous of me because I was the oldest son and Poppa favored me," Pias mused. "Jealousy can twist even the most decent people into monsters. Perhaps he felt so insecure that he had to get me out of the way, and when that didn't make him feel any better he got nastier and more cruel, hoping that more and more power would fill the vacuum in his soul. But no amount of power can do that; a soul has to be healed from the inside, not from the outside."

Pias sighed. "Oh hell, I'm no psychologist. I don't know if that's what's wrong with him or not. There's something dreadfully sick within him, I saw that the last time I was home—but what caused it, when it began, and what can be done about it . . . I just don't know."

"He has to be stopped," Beti said with gritty determination. "That's why I came to find you. You've always been able to stand up to him, all the time I was growing up. You're the only person he's really afraid of, you're the only one who could take control away from him. Legally, as oldest son. . . ."

"Legally I'm not the oldest son," Pias said bitterly.

"Legally, according to the *kriss*, I'm nobody. I don't exist. Nobody on Newforest will have anything to do with me."

"A lot of people are beginning to realize they made a mistake," Beti said. "They want you to come back and put Tas in his place. They want you as the next duke. They're even making up songs about you, about the wandering son who'll come back one day and save Newforest from tyranny."

Pias turned his face away. "It's not that easy, Beti. I've made a new life for myself here. The reasons I had for leaving Newforest, the things I couldn't explain to the *kriss*, are still there and even now I can't tell you about them. I have responsibilities to something far greater than the welfare of a single world. I don't know if I'll ever be able to return. I don't know if I'll want to. I had to turn off so much of myself to keep it from hurting. To bring it back now. . . ." He shivered at the thought.

"I understand," Beti said, her voice like a little girl's. "We turned our backs on you and cast you out. We have no right to ask you for favors now."

She sighed. "I guess I'm in the same boat now. I'll have to change my name and find somewhere safe to live."

This jolted Pias out of his own unhappy thoughts. "Huh? Why?" He turned to face her again.

"I can't go back home, not after this. You were my one hope, and now that's gone."

Something inside Pias went cold and brittle. "You mean it was *Tas* who tried to kill you? His own sister?"

"He keeps the whole family under lock and key; he's afraid we'll challenge him and get people to back us. We're not in chains, but we've got some of his 'escorts' wherever we go to make sure we don't do anything wrong. Old Yuri helped me escape in a wagonload of mulaska melons. I had barely enough money to book passage on a couple of ships, first to Belange, then to Wallach, and finally I caught the freighter coming here, hoping to find you. I don't know how he tracked me

down, but those must have been some of his men who
. . . who. . . ."

She broke into fresh tears, and Pias held her tightly
once more. But as his hands tenderly caressed her shoulders his face hardened into an expression of grim determination. As Beti's sobbing subsided once more, he
whispered, "I can't let him get away with that. I can't
let him do it—not to you, not to them, though God
knows they've deserved it."

He pushed Beti away slightly so he could look into her
face. "I have the Empire on one side and you and the
family and Newforest on the other. But I can't sit by
and let my family be murdered by my power-mad
brother. That's not in anyone's interest, not even the
Empress's."

He sighed.

Then he moved apart from her, and his tone was all
business. "Tell me what's happened since I left. Tell me
everything, every detail no matter how small. If I'm
going to be of any help, I have to know what I'm facing."

After hearing his sister's story and assuring her she'd
be safe with Baron Ebert, Pias took Yvonne with him to
police headquarters where the would-be assassins were
being held. With the word of the baron backing them
up, they gained quick admittance to the killers.

Even under detrazine, though, it was clear that Beti's
attackers could give them little additional information.
They were low-level blasterbats, local criminals hired
by an anonymous voice over the vidiphone—with the
visual circuits blanked out—to perform the specific task
of killing Beti Bavol. They were told precisely where she
was staying and that they should perform their task as
quickly as possible. They didn't know who had hired
them or whether there was any connection with the
planet Newforest.

Disappointed, the two SOTE agents flew back to
Felicité, discussing the problem along the way. "From
what Beti told me," Pias said, "Tas has revolutionized

21

the planet singlehanded. It was always a rather back-ward, easygoing place; now he's brought in computer-ized equipment, he's spying on his citizens, he's even building factories. That's much too institutionalized for good old Newforest. If it were just the factories and the computers, I could excuse it as an attempt to bring 'progress' to the planet—but the ruthless way he's going about it makes it different somehow. Something's hap-pening there, something . . . well, I hate to say 'evil,' it sounds so melodramatic, but that's the feeling I get. Something evil has gripped Newforest and won't let go. What I don't understand is why the local SOTE office hasn't reported anything about this.''

"Maybe they have," Vonnie said. "The Empress gives local nobility a great deal of leeway—it's the only way an empire of this scale can survive. Her father tried to avoid meddling in local matters as much as possible, and Edna seems to be following that same policy. She and the Head may be waiting to see just how far this will go before they step in.''

"When it goes as far as murder, that's too far.''

"I agree, and something will have to be done. The thing I don't understand is how your brother was able to track Beti down so quickly. Within hours of her arrival the killers knew exactly where to find her. That would be understandable on Newforest, where he probably has lots of spies, but on a distant planet it's much harder to trace someone. He must have some organization behind him.''

The implications of her statement remained floating in the air between them, but neither agent voiced them aloud. Instead they flew the rest of the way back to the d'Alembert estate in brooding silence.

As soon as they reached Felicité, Pias put through a subcom call to the Head's private number on Earth. Grand Duke Zander von Wilmenhorst, the chief of the Service of the Empire, was unavailable at the moment, but Pias spoke to his daughter and prime lieutenant, Helena. He asked for a leave of absence to settle some family matters, and described to her in some detail what he'd learned of events on Newforest. Helena listened somberly as she considered the situation.

"I don't recall any strongly negative reports from Newforest," she said when Pias was done, "and I see virtually all the reports that come in. I see so many reports it makes my eyes ache."

She closed her eyes and tried to concentrate. "As far as I can recall, the only thing that's come in about Newforest was that they were making a big push toward modernization. Nothing wrong with that, so we haven't paid much attention. If what your sister says is true, someone is lying to us somewhere down the line—possibly someone in the Service office itself. I don't like that one bit."

She paused and looked straight at Pias. "What you're describing doesn't sound to me like a leave of absence at all. It sounds like a full-blown assignment, to investigate illegal and treasonous activities on Newforest and to take steps to correct the situation. You don't have to ask permission to do that."

"There are personal matters involved," Pias said, "and I didn't want to just disappear on you if you had any other assignments for me."

"I understand the personal matters very well," Helena said, her expression softening suddenly. "Newforest is your home, and should have been your inheritance. I know the depth of your concern. *You* know, though, that the d'Alembert teams have a standing assignment to investigate anything that looks suspicious to them—unless they're given something specific to do instead. Right now, everything's quiet—everyone's holding their breath to see what turns out in the Omicron situation. You're free to pursue any investigations that strike your fancy. I appreciate knowing where you'll be, in case of trouble. I'll notify the local office there to stand by to give you any assistance. . . ."

"That might not be such a wise idea," Vonnie said, "in view of the fact that someone there might be falsifying the reports."

Helena winced. "You're right, of course. It makes me

23

shudder just to think there might be traitors in the Service; it was bad enough when we had to weed out so many during the Banion mess. Find out what you can, and if it calls for official action we can bring in help from the outside.

"If things are as bad as your sister claims, you won't have to go into much detail; just give us a preliminary report. You're a good investigator and troubleshooter, but we've got specialists in planetary administration who can handle the mop-up once you've pointed them in the right direction. There's no need to risk yourself unnecessarily on a minor housekeeping matter like this; the Service needs your talents too much for major projects."

But to Pias Bavol this was far more than "a minor housekeeping matter." This was his family, and Newforest was the planet he'd once hoped to inherit. Unimportant though it might be in the scheme of galactic history, this was his home and his people—and even though he was sorely tempted to let the friends and family who'd betrayed him suffer the consequences of their actions, he vowed to put into this case every bit of energy it took to set the situation right again.

CHAPTER 3

Return to Newforest

Pias had a major battle on his hands even before he left
DesPlaines. Yvonne d'Alembert—impatient at her enforced idleness and nervous about the fate of her spouse
—demanded to accompany him on his trip to Newforest. It would at least give her something to do to take
her mind off Jules's dangerous assignment on Omicron.

Pias at first protested that the children would be left
unattended, to which Vonnie replied that there were
plenty of servants on the vast ducal estate, as well as the
Marchioness Gabrielle—and if they got tired of watching the children, Vonnie's father was always eager to see
them. "I refuse to be thought of as the weak link in this
family," she insisted. "I'm always the one who has to
stay behind, and it just isn't fair. I can pull my weight
with the rest of you."

Pias agreed that was so, but voiced a new objection.
"This is a job that calls for a great deal of subtlety," he
said, "and I'm afraid you'd stand out too much."

"Thanks a lot!" Vonnie grimaced. "I'm as good
at undercover work as anyone in this family. I was taking classes before you ever thought to leave Newforest,

and I got a 989 on the Thousand Point Test. That's not exactly spaceslime, *tovarishch*."

Pias shook his head as he tried to soothe his sister-in-law's temper. "I didn't mean to imply you weren't any good, but Newforest is a special case. We stayed isolated from the rest of the Empire until two generations ago. We've got a language of our own and a very distinct culture. Outsiders are viewed with great suspicion and distrust, and it would take you weeks, maybe even months, to learn everything you'd need to be able to pass for a native. I just can't afford the delay. If Tas would try to kill Beti, who knows what he'll do to the rest of the family—or to the rest of Newforest. I've got to stop him quickly."

The argument continued, but in the end Pias was victorious. He would travel to Newforest alone and investigate his brother's activities. He did promise that if any action were to be taken he would notify Yvonne as well as SOTE Headquarters on Earth, giving his sister-in-law a chance to get in on the adventure.

Pias left for Newforest a few hours later in one of the small private ships the d'Alembert family kept at Felicité's spacefield. It was a long trip from DesPlaines to Newforest, and Pias had plenty of time to consider the strategy he would use in his investigation.

The first thing he would have to do was disguise himself. As a young marquis and heir to the planet, he had always been a popular figure and his appearance was well known to most of the populace. By the edict of the *kriss*, the council of elders, he was a nonperson and anyone who saw him was supposed to treat him as though he didn't exist. That would make it hard to obtain any information from the people about what was really happening on Newforest. Even worse, Pias was afraid that someone recognizing him would inform Tas, and then he'd be in trouble.

To avoid that problem he dyed his sandy brown hair a deep black, changed his hairline with plucking and growth inhibitors, used skin pigments to darken his complexion, and applied a thick mustache to his normally bare upper lip. He inserted contact lenses to change his eye color from blue to brown. For hours he practiced speaking in a voice that was higher and more nasal than his usual tones, and he gave himself a trace of a country accent that would label him as coming from well outside the capital city of Garridan where the Bavol family made its home.

Landing on Newforest would be awkward. Because of its high gravity, no one went there casually—and because it had little heavy industry or interstellar trade, the planet attracted even fewer visitors than DesPlaines did. Anyone landing at the spaceport was an immediate object of suspicion—and particularly so if he arrived in a personal spaceship. Very few Newforesters could afford their own private ships; landing at Garridan Spaceport would attract undue attention—something an undercover agent preferred to avoid.

Pias would have to land somewhere unofficially. There was a range of hills about thirty kilometers south of the town where he thought he might come down unseen. He hated the thought of walking so far into town, but he could think of no alternative. Meanwhile, in preparation, he went through the ship as thoroughly as he could, removing anything that might identify it. If someone spotted it while he was gone, he didn't want to leave any clues pointing to himself or, worse, to the d'Alemberts of DesPlaines. He'd also brought along some cases of expensive perfume and some mildly pornographic sensable tapes; if planetary officials examined the ship, they'd think he was a smuggler, not a spy.

He'd thought a secret landing would be easily arranged. Garridan was not a busy port and its detection equipment was largely unsophisticated. Since there was no naval base there either, there should have been no detectors capable of spotting his small craft—or, if they did spot him, there would be no resources for tracking him down and following him to his landing site. He would be at most a momentary enigma that would fade from their memories almost as fast as he faded from their sensor screens.

His ship emerged from subspace about twenty million

kilometers out from Newforest and quickly began spiraling in. His troubles began just before he reached the uppermost levels of the planet's atmosphere. An official radio announcement demanded that he identify himself immediately or face legal action. Pias ignored the warning and concentrated on plotting a course to land at his chosen hiding site.

The warning came a second time, and Pias suddenly noticed two ships on his sensor screen coming up to intercept him. Newforest had never had a big problem with smugglers, and no one ever wanted to land here illegally, so the government had never bothered to challenge ships before. He cursed himself for not expecting a fight after everything Beti had told him about Tas's security crackdown, but it was still hard for him to think of his home world as anything but easygoing. In the back of his mind, Pias knew that such measures meant there was something on Newforest that required guarding from prying eyes. But that was a consideration for later; right now, he had some evasive action to take.

He wasn't much worried about the two ships themselves. He'd naturally be careful, for either of them would have the firepower to blow his own small vessel out of the ether, but he'd evaded more thorough opposition in the past. The real threat would be from the organization behind those fighters. Newforest was now a planet on guard against intruders, and that would make his mission infinitely more dangerous.

The attackers began firing at him even before the second warning was finished, but by that time Pias already had his craft in motion. The vessel dipped and rolled and twisted as his hands played across the ship's controls, and the fighters trying to intercept him were slow to respond; apparently they were not as accustomed to combat situations as he was—and Pias was still a rank amateur compared to his brother-in-law Jules. The security systems on Newforest must still be comparatively new, then, and the pilots unpracticed in their roles. That gave him some hope of success.

Pias's ship darted and wove an intricate pattern through the upper levels of Newforest's atmosphere, and the interceptors followed awkwardly behind him. At first Pias did not return their fire, waiting to see how serious the situation would become. When no more attack ships rose from the planet's surface to chase him, he guessed that the pair were all Tas had at the moment.

When he was sure there'd be no further opposition, Pias turned on the automatic weaponry. Spaceship battles were haphazard affairs because of the relative motions of all parties through three dimensions, and the computer-guided weapons were never as effective as an experienced human gunner because they couldn't be as intuitive. Pias would have liked nothing better than to have his beloved Yvette there to fire at the enemy—but since she wasn't there and he couldn't handle the guns and the controls at the same time, he had to let the machines do his fighting for him.

As it turned out, his ship's computers were more than a match for their opposition, who were less adept at dodging than Pias was. Within a very few minutes both ships had been disabled and their pilots had to radio for help. Pias was able to resume his landing unopposed.

He did not delude himself into thinking he was now safe, however; if Newforest had equipment sophisticated enough to spot his little ship in the first place, they would also track him to his landing spot. Soon after touchdown the ship would be surrounded by Tas's security force. He'd have to get away quickly to avoid being trapped in their net.

He began altering his plans. The hills he'd originally selected were too far away from town, and his reason for picking them was no longer valid. Landing there now would handicap him; he'd have to scramble across hilly terrain while his pursuers could track him comfortably in copters.

He began looking at the more inhabited regions closer to Garridan. Newforest was such an underpopulated world that there were still large tracts of undeveloped land near even the largest cities, and as he came lower Pias was able to spot an area that looked suitable—a scattered woodland near the edge of a large pond, with many small farms scattered between the woods and the capital city. The woods would give him cover as he left the ship, and the farms would provide plenty of places to hide if pursuit came after him. Once in Garridan itself, he had no doubts at all about his ability to blend in and disappear.

The landing was tricky—first, because he was having to alter his course from moment to moment to select the best spot, and second, because he didn't have the help of ground traffic control to guide him in. He'd never made such an impromptu landing in his brief experience as a spaceship pilot—and the problem was further complicated by Newforest's heavy gravity. Fortunately, he'd learned his landing procedures on DesPlaines, and he was able to compensate.

The ground came up to meet him almost before he was ready, and he had to fire the braking rockets hard to control his descent. There was really no clearing big enough for his ship; he'd have to create one the hard way. His vessel hit the trees with considerable force, chopping off upper limbs and pushing aside the thick trunks.

His ship landed with a tooth-jarring thump. Because of its odd position within the woods, with trees pressing against it on two sides, it began to tilt over immediately upon touchdown. Pias quickly turned off all power systems to avoid possible explosions, leaving just enough for the lights and air regeneration systems. He held his breath, afraid to move, as the ship's cant increased, and finally relaxed as the nose came to rest against another tree. The little vessel was in a terrible position, but at least it would fall no further.

Pias unstrapped himself from the acceleration couch. He was glad he'd prepared everything ahead of time on the long flight here from DesPlaines, and had made the ship look like a smuggler's vessel; with Tas's defenses alerted, he'd have less time to get away from here than he'd planned, and every second was crucial.

He staggered awkwardly through the oddly sloping corridors of the ship to the airlock, and faced an unexpected problem: how to get down. The normal boarding ramp was jammed. It was about a three-story drop to the forest floor—hazardous even in one gee and possibly fatal in Newforest's two-and-a-half gees.

There was no time to look for fancy solutions. Pias reached for the handholds in the ship's hull and began lowering himself down the side even though, at this angle, it meant he was climbing almost horizontally, with Newforest's heavy gravity tugging at his back trying to make him fall. The magnisteel hull dissipated heat quickly, but the handholds were still very hot from the atmospheric friction of the landing, and Pias's hands stung from their tight grip on the hot metal. When he reached a point only a few meters above the ground he decided to risk the drop, and fell the rest of the way. Landing the way he'd been trained, he rolled to his feet unhurt and took stock of the situation.

It had been only a few minutes since his ship came to rest, yet already he could hear the whirr of approaching copters that signaled pursuit. Again the small curious voice in the back of his mind wondered what was suddenly so special about Newforest that warranted such thorough protection from prying eyes. There was enough firepower in his ship to blast any copters out of the sky and Pias had enough weaponry on his body to put up a significant fight, but that wasn't his objective. He'd come to Newforest to observe the situation, not to engage in military battles. He'd already made a bigger splash than he'd intended; Tas would be on the lookout for an intruder, making Pias's undercover job that much harder. Taking a stand here would only strengthen the defense's resolve; a smuggler, as he was trying to portray himself, would much prefer to run and hide until they relaxed a little bit.

It was late afternoon in this part of the world. Pias quickly oriented himself by the dim red sun and started off in a southerly direction, toward Garridan. He moved as cautiously as he could, trying not to leave too obvious a trail for his followers to spot, but speed was his primary consideration. If Tas was as thorough about this line of defense as he was about the others, there would be infrared and other sophisticated scanners that could spot his fleeing figure without the need to look for broken branches to mark his passage. He wanted to be as far from the ship as possible so they'd have to search an area with a large radius.

Because the plant life of Newforest took its energy from the rays of a red sun, the local equivalent of chlorophyll was a substance that reflected back light most strongly in the red-orange portion of the spectrum. As a result, much of the vegetation looked as though it were stained with blood in the late afternoon light. Having grown up on Newforest, Pias gave no thought to the eeriness of this scene as he pushed his way through the brush; his only concern was to get away from the ship and the pursuit that would inevitably follow.

Small animals scattered before him as he ran, which was all to the good; the more movement there was in the forest, the more it would confuse the enemy sensors. Pias heard the copters pass near his position, and held still for a moment until they went by. The copters would go first to the ship and search it for clues; failing to find any, they'd start a wide sweep of the area in an effort to cut him off.

The forest was starting to thin out, and Pias realized he must be coming to its southern edge. Beyond the woods would be open field and he dared not let himself be caught out there. Even at night he'd be obvious to his adversaries' scanners.

As he came to the edge of the woods he paralleled the line of trees moving around toward the east until he spotted a small farmhouse and barn a few hundred meters away. That looked like his best bet. If he could reach that habitation, he could probably hide until much of the fuss had died down. Then it would be merely a matter of taking the road into Garridan, pretending to be someone from the country who was visiting the planetary capital for the first time. Tas's police would be on the lookout for a smuggler, so he hoped he could make that story stick well enough to fool them.

He edged through the woods until he came to the spot nearest the farm buildings. He could hear the search copters circling again and knew they were looking for him, but they were way off to the southwest; with any luck they wouldn't cover this area until he was well hidden. He checked to make sure there was no one in the farmyard who could see him, then dashed across open ground until he reached the side of the barn. He soon found an open door and slipped inside.

The barn was dark and smelled strongly of animals —of bullards, the slow-witted draft animals that still pulled plows in the less technological rural areas, and of cartlies, the lighter, faster animals that pulled wagons and carts for transportation. The animals rustled nervously as they caught the scent of a strange human, but they sent up no alarm. Pias looked around and saw no one. So far he was still safe.

He would have to stay here at least until after dark, possibly longer. It would all depend on how vigorous a search the security forces made for the smuggler. He might have to spend the entire night and try to leave in the morning.

Pias moved quietly through the barn until he found a small compartment where harnesses and tools were stored. Squeezing in, he folded himself up as comfortably as he could and tried to rest. He'd done a lot of running already and might be called on to do some more; he might as well take advantage of this respite while he could.

He must have dozed off, because he woke with a jolt. He strained his senses to learn what had awakened him, but the barn seemed quiet outside the cramped confines of his hiding place. Then he heard a sound—the slow creaking of the barn door on its hinges. Someone had come in here very quietly. That person obviously knew something was amiss.

Pias tried to reach for the stun-gun inside his vest, but the closeness of the compartment made it impossible to bend his elbow the proper way. In any case, the gesture would have been futile, for he suddenly found himself staring down the barrel of a stun-rifle. A deep masculine voice said, "Come on out of there before I have to shoot you."

CHAPTER 4

Tas the Tyrant

Even staring down the barrel of a weapon, Pias remained cool and rational. This stun-rifle was at least twenty years old; they didn't make models of this particular shape any more. If Tas was upgrading his security forces, he'd hardly give them outmoded weaponry. Then too, the man's words had been stern, but scarcely officious. This was no man of a military mind barking crisp orders. Pias guessed he was facing the owner of this small farm, who was concerned with a trespasser on his property.

Moving carefully, so he wouldn't alarm his captor, Pias squeezed out of the storage compartment. He kept his hands up and well away from his body; the farmer was probably more nervous than he was, and Pias didn't want to make any mistakes that would frighten the man into shooting without cause.

As he'd guessed, the man was dressed casually in country work clothes—but he knew how to hold a gun. "Who are you?" the farmer asked, never taking his sights off Pias. His voice had a thick rural flavor as he spoke Romny, the native tongue of Newforest.

"My name's Gari Nav, and I mean you no harm," Pias replied in the voice he'd practiced aboard the ship.

"What were you doing in there?"

"Sleeping," Pias answered truthfully. "It's a little cramped, but it's good and dark."

"Why were you in there?"

"I'm not a thief, if that's what you're thinking. I was just looking for someplace where I wouldn't disturb anyone for a while, then I'd go along my way."

The farmer didn't lower his gun. "That's not an explanation."

The sound of a copter grew louder overhead. "But that is," Pias said, looking up to indicate the sound from above.

A teenage boy poked his head in through the door. "Poppa, it's the brassies. They're landing in the front yard."

The farmer looked sternly at Pias. "What do they want with you?"

Pias was taking a gamble, and he knew it—but he also knew the Newforest people. They were mostly descendents of Gypsies and English Tinkers who had fled Earth during the bad years of the early twenty-first century. They hated authority and loved a clever rogue— and Pias hoped he could capitalize on that fact now that he was facing a threat from the planetary authorities.

"I was just trying to make a profit with some off-world goods," Pias said with a wink. "The government's mad because I don't have an import license."

The farmer had a hard decision to make, and he had to make it quickly. The "brassies," as Tas's security agents were evidently called, had brought their copters down and their footsteps could be plainly heard walking toward the barn. He had to make up his mind whether he believed Pias's story and, if he did, whether it was enough to keep him from turning the fugitive in.

"Get back in there," the farmer said, motioning at the storage compartment with the barrel of his rifle. "We'll sort this out later."

Pias hastened to comply. He was not out of danger

yet, but the farmer had shown the expected tendency to prefer the individual over the police. Now all he had to do was hope the police *behaved* like police. Nothing would more insure his winning the farmer's sympathy than highhanded behavior from the security forces.

As soon as Pias was out of sight the farmer walked to the barn door where he was met by the leader of the security team. Pias could not see what was happening from his hiding place, but the sound of their voices reached him well enough.

"Are you the owner here?" the security leader asked, and her voice was so brisk and businesslike it made Pias smile. She would do a splendid job of alienating the farmer and shifting his sympathies toward Pias.

"Yes," the farmer answered tersely.

"Have you seen any strangers around?"

"Is there any trouble?"

"I'll ask the questions, you answer them."

"Ain't seen no one I'd call a stranger," the farmer said. "We're pretty out of the way; don't get many visitors."

"What about you? Is your card in order?"

"Should be, I don't use it much."

"Let me see it."

"It's in the house."

The security leader fumed. "You're supposed to carry it with you at all times."

"I did, at first, but I got out of the habit. My bullards all recognize me by sight."

"Just get it and stop trying to be clever."

The footsteps walked away from the barn toward the small farmhouse, and Pias could no longer hear what was going on. He waited in suspense for an agonizingly long time until finally he heard the copters take off once more. A few minutes after that, when they were no longer in range, he could hear the barn door swing open again and the farmer called to him, "You can come out again."

Pias did so and found that the farmer still had the rifle handy. He might distrust the authorities, but that

36

didn't mean he automatically trusted Pias.

"I know I've brought you trouble, and I'm sorry for it," Pias apologized sincerely. "I'd like to pay you for letting me stay here for the night, and for dinner, too, if you can spare it. Tomorrow morning I'll be on my way and you needn't bother about me again."

"We don't take money for hospitality here," the farmer said. His rifle was no longer pointed directly at Pias, but he kept it tucked in the crook of his arm just in case. Pias knew that the stubbornness of the Newforest people would keep the man from acknowledging friendship for a while yet—but he also knew the extent of his own charm and was confident the man and his family would be on his side before the evening was out.

The farmer's name, Pias discovered, was Mestipen Smitt and his wife was Klarika. They had five children and earned a decent living here on the farm, enough to suit their modest needs. Pias offered to help with the evening chores and his enthusiastic hard work finally convinced Smitt that he was no threat to the family and was entitled to come into the house as company rather than as a prisoner.

The Smitt family accepted Pias into their home with all the generosity of which Newforesters were capable. Klarika fixed him a delicious meal and refused his offer of payment. As the family sat around the dinner table, Pias's gentle probing brought forth a picture of recent life on Newforest.

A few years ago the government had declared a policy of "modernization." Though the statement was issued in the duke's name, everyone knew that Tas Bavol—the heir to all of Newforest now that his older brother Pias had been banished—was really running the show. Taxes immediately tripled, but the benefits did not increase correspondingly. All the citizens had received for their money was an oppressive government that was more computerized, more centralized. Every citizen was issued a special identification card different from the standard imperial ID card; he was supposed to carry this new card with him wherever he went, and had to produce it to authorities on demand or face a stiff jail sentence. In the course of just a few months, Newforest had gone from being one of the most unstructured societies in the Empire to being one of the most authoritarian.

These changes did not sit well with the normally easygoing populace. The name of Tas Bavol was seldom spoken these days without spitting. Even though Pias was technically a nonperson who'd been erased from people's memories, there were still references to him as "the lost one," and not a few wistful thoughts that he might return some day, somehow, to rid Newforest of its troubles. Still, people didn't say such things too openly, for one of the things Tas had bought with all the new taxes was an efficient new security force, complete with crisp brown uniforms and shiny brass buttons that gave the agents their nickname of "brassies." Opposition to the new regime was quickly silenced, and some of its severest critics had simply disappeared, never to be seen again.

Pias was not at liberty to ask too many direct questions without compromising his cover identity, but he couldn't help wondering how such a setup could come about within the empire ruled by such a just figure as Empress Stanley Eleven. A *laissez-faire* policy was all very well in the abstract, but it had been taken to great extremes here on his home world—and Pias wanted to know why.

The Smitts insisted that Pias sleep in the house rather than the barn as he was willing to do, and again refused his offer of payment for their generosity. The next morning when he needed transportation into Garridan, Pias insisted on buying the cartly and wagon rig he'd need, rather than taking it from the Smitts on an indefinite loan. He made sure the price he gave them was more than fair to compensate for their generosity and helpfulness.

Pias set out along the road at a leisurely pace, in keeping with his disguise as a country fellow visiting the big city for the first time. Klarika Smitt had given him a hearty breakfast and packed a substantial lunch for him to eat along the way; were it not for his worry about what was happening to his native world, Pias would have been as carefree as he appeared to be. He saw copters circling the area a couple of times, but his rig looked like such a perfectly natural part of the New-forest landscape that they did not question his right to be where he was.

It was late in the day when he finally reached the capital city. For all Tas's "modernization," Garridan looked scarcely changed. There were a few new buildings in the skyline, but still none over four stories tall—a very practical consideration on a high-gee world. The city—which was really more like a town—was still only a few dozen square kilometers in area and retained its essentially rustic character. Most of the traffic in the streets was mechanized, but cartly-drawn vehicles were still prevalent enough to be unexceptional. It all made for interesting traffic problems, and motorists in Garridan had frequent occasion to curse the slow-moving beasts that blocked the intersections.

The dirt road Pias had been following became a paved one at the outskirts of the city, and it was here he encountered a roadblock. At first he was worried that it had been set up especially to capture the intruder, but then he saw that it was of a more permanent nature. This checkpoint kept tabs on all traffic going in and out of the city, and would not specifically try to trip him up. Even a routine check could be trouble if it were set up properly, though, so he had to remain alert.

He pulled his wagon up to the roadblock and stopped obediently at the officer's order. "What's your name?" the policeman asked brusquely.

"Gari Nav, if it please you, sir."

"What's your business in Garridan?"

"I just want to visit and see the sights. Been living out in the hills all my life and decided it was time to see something of the world."

This answer did not sit well with the officer. Anything that did not fit within the narrow confines of his experience was a potential trouble spot. "Let me see your card."

"What card?"

"Your citizen's card."

"I don't have any card."

"Everybody has a card."

"Not me," Pias said with naive simplicity.

"Citizen's cards were issued to everyone on Newforest over the age of ten."

"Then they must've missed me, because I never got one."

The officer fumed and spoke a few words into his wristcom. After a moment instructions came back and he spoke again to Pias. "You're to leave your wagon here and come with me," he insisted. Pias obeyed with outward cheerfulness, though his innards were tensed for battle at any moment.

Pias was searched thoroughly, but had fortunately taken the precaution of burying his weapons a short distance outside town. It left him feeling somehow naked and helpless, but considering the police-state mentality that now prevailed on Newforest, it was better than being caught with unregistered weapons. Guns would be useless in this initial police confrontation. If he survived this, weapons could be obtained easily enough in the city if one knew where to look for them.

Having determined that Pias was unarmed, the policeman put him in a car and drove him down to the central police headquarters—a building that had been substantially improved since Pias's last visit to Newforest. With little reported crime on Newforest, the police had always been a formality that no one, least of all themselves, took very seriously. All that had changed, and Pias found himself in the middle of a busy, efficient office where people in their spotless uniforms moved briskly about their urgent tasks. The faces were humorless, the atmosphere heavy and solemn.

Pias was taken into a stark office and seated in front of a desk, where a higher-ranking officer questioned him for over an hour about his background. Pias stuck to the story he'd invented for himself—that he lived on a small farm up in the hills and had few dealings with civilization. He hunted or grew most of his own food, trading with neighbors for the few other things he needed. No one had ever come to his farm to give him a citizen's card and he'd never heard about them until today. His tone was unfailingly polite and helpful without giving the police anything they could use against him.

The police were especially suspicious because the unknown intruder was still at large, but Pias was so obviously a native of Newforest that he managed to allay most of their doubts. In the end, they decided to issue him a citizen's card and consider the matter closed. Pias was fingerprinted and had his retinal patterns recorded; all that and more information about him was encoded on the small blue plastic card they gave him. He was told to keep the card with him at all times and then driven back to the roadblock, where he picked up his wagon and was allowed to enter Garridan officially.

Pias had brought plenty of money with him, and spent a week living in Garridan, growing more and more alarmed by what he saw. The citizen's card was a necessity on Newforest; not only did the police have the right to stop anyone at random on the street and ask to see the card, but it was impossible to buy anything without presenting the card at the time of purchase. From renting a hotel room to eating meals to buying basic toiletries, there was virtually no aspect of life that was not controlled or regulated by that simple blue card.

More alarming than that, though, was the attitude of the people. Newforest had always been a lighthearted world, and the inhabitants of Garridan had been noted for their easy informal ways. Now there was a pall of fear over the town. People were particularly careful about what they said and to whom they said it, and invariably looked over their shoulders before speaking to make sure no police were in the area. People spoke in whispers in dark corners; Pias, as a stranger in town,

41

was excluded from most conversations, though there there had been a time when even strangers shared in the activities of Garridan. Nowadays, no one could afford to trust someone he didn't know.

Out of curiosity, Pias took a walk by the local office of the Service of the Empire. Because Newforest was an out-of-the-way planet where little ever happened, the SOTE office was barely more than a storefront staffed by a couple of low-level officials. Pias considered going in, but thought better of it when he saw the trio of police officers loitering nearby. They were watching the office and obviously prepared to take note of anyone trying to contact SOTE with complaints about the local regime. Pias had little doubt that calls to SOTE were also monitored, further discouraging local complaints. Still, such activities should not have silenced the SOTE operatives themselves; anyone with eyes could see what a reprehensible situation was occurring here. SOTE's failure to do anything indicated a tremendous breakdown somewhere in the system.

Pias spent a week in Garridan, becoming more and more depressed at the dismal circumstances. He wandered, watched, listened, and spent a good deal of time mentally composing the blistering report he would write to the Head. But the report was still incomplete; there were still things he had to discover about Tas and the way the system operated.

The key to everything on Newforest seemed to be those little blue citizen's cards. Through their use, a person could be tracked throughout the city and his movements monitored to a high degree of precision. Pias's own trail had been innocent and random; the security forces would learn nothing by keeping track of where he went and what he did. But there was serious potential for abuse; with a system this tight, individual freedom became purely a rhetorical concept.

To make the system work would require an enormous degree of computer sophistication, a reliance on technology that Pias would have thought antithetical to the Newforest character. Somewhere there had to be a computer facility where this random information, compiled from all over the world, was assimilated and analyzed to look for troublemakers or signs of rebellion. There had been no major computer centers on Newforest when Pias had left it. Somehow, Tas had built one in the last few years to consolidate his tyrannical rule. Such a facility would have needed outside help to build—and Pias was almost afraid to speculate on where that help could have come from.

It didn't take Pias long to find the center. There was only one place in Garridan that was both new enough and large enough to house such a mammoth facility: a sprawling, heavily guarded installation near the outskirts of town. The number of guards around it, and the fact that the outside was kept brightly lit around the clock, indicated its importance to Tas's regime. It was so thoroughly watched that it became an irresistible target of Pias's curiosity.

Many agents would simply have reported the buildings as suspicious and left it to an official Service team of experts to investigate the inside. But going through channels might give Tas time to cover up the true nature of his operation. Pias felt he had to go inside and take at least a preliminary look around. He was not a computer expert and was not sure he could spot something significant even if it was right in front of him, but comparing the place before and after an official SOTE investigation would at least show whether changes had been made.

The building was so well guarded that Pias knew he had no chance of making a surreptitious entrance. Only uniformed guards and people with special clearances were allowed in and out of the place. Pias would have to disguise himself as one or the other. After some brief thought, he decided to impersonate one of the brassies. A uniform, by its very nature, was made to be taken for granted. One person in uniform looked very much like another and unless his fingerprints or retinal pattern were checked, Pias could probably walk through many areas of the building unchallenged.

He haunted the area near the time of shift change and

followed one of the guards who was near his own size as the man got off work. Pias tracked him patiently until the man passed a deserted alleyway, where the SOTE agent promptly waylaid him. The man was no match for Pias's Service training, and within minutes Pias found himself in possession of a uniform and a blaster—and a security badge that cleared him to pass through the gates of the computer complex. By taking this action he realized he was limiting himself. The guard's absence would be noticed within a day, or thirty-six hours at most; Pias would have to be well away before then. Still, the chance to look around inside the complex seemed worth the risk.

He tied up his victim, donned the uniform, and strode purposefully back to the guarded installation. The guards at the front gate barely gave him a second glance as he casually flashed his security pass at them. In like manner Pias passed two other checkpoints before entering the front door of the building itself.

Inside, the structure was even bigger than it looked from the exterior. The planet's heavy gravity dictated how tall a building could be above ground level, but there was no such limit on how deep into the earth it could extend. The complex was a tall one for Newforest, rising three stories above the ground. It sank at least twice that many below ground. The computer facility was a small city in itself, housing hundreds of workers who tended the machines and analyzed the data pouring in continuously from all parts of the planet.

Pias could not stand around and gawk, or it would destroy his cover; as a uniformed guard, he was supposed to be quite familiar with all this. With so many people in constant motion he wasn't noticed as he walked briskly in a random direction, pretending he knew precisely where he was going. He kept his eyes open for clues about what was happening where, and no one stopped him or questioned his presence in this supposedly sacrosanct installation.

At last he saw a sign pointing the way to the administrative section, and decided that was where he would get some of the information he was seeking. As it was the night shift, most of the administrative personnel were gone, their offices and desks empty. Pias wandered through the aisles and past another security checkpoint until he came to the chief administrative officer's room. The door was locked. Pias could spot no special alarm system; a short beam from his blaster burned out the mechanism and he entered the room unseen.

The desk top, with a computer scanner built into it, was barren of paper; apparently most of the work was stored in the computer itself with little need for printout. Still, Pias had never heard of any operation that didn't use some hard copy, and he began searching the desk drawers.

A slight noise made him stop and reach for the blaster at his hip, but as he looked up, he realized the gesture was futile. Standing in the doorway to the room was his brother Tas, holding a blaster already pointed at his chest—and behind Tas was a small army of brassies, all similarly armed.

"Hello, Pias," Tas said with all the false warmth of a fourth-rate undertaker. "Welcome home."

But it was not his brother's words, nor the blaster, that attracted most of Pias's attention. Around Tas's neck, almost hidden by his collar, was a thin silver chain from which dangled a single integrated circuit chip—the recognition symbol of the conspiracy that was out to overthrow the Empire. Pias's worst fears were suddenly realized: Tas Bavol had sold his soul, and the entire planet of Newforest, to the Empire's worst enemy.

CHAPTER 5

The Resurrection of Pias Bavol

"I wish I could say it was good to see you again," Pias replied in even tones. As he spoke, his mind raced. Tas might not know that Pias was now an agent of SOTE, or that he'd had special training. For all he knew, Pias had returned at Beti's request, to undermine Tas's authority. As long as he thought that, there was a chance Pias could somehow talk his way out of the situation—but if Tas ever learned that he represented the Service, Pias was not likely to survive the revelation.

"Yes, you never liked me," Tas sneered.

"I always treated you fairly."

"Of course—big brother generously doling out the crumbs. I got tired of a steady diet of crumbs. I wanted the whole loaf, and now I've got it."

"And are you happy now that you've got what you want, now that you've enslaved our whole planet?"

"You always were the romantic," Tas said. "The truth is far less melodramatic than you make it seem. Newforest was a sleepy, backwater place with nothing to recommend it. I'm merely yanking it into the twenty-fifth century, preparing it for its proper place in galactic affairs. I'm making it strong, Pias. Naturally people are complaining, the same way your muscles complain when you exercise them, to build up your body. Change always hurts. The whole Empire is in for a change soon and a lot of people will be hurt—but the Empire will be a stronger place afterward."

If I'm a romantic, you're a true believer, Pias thought. *You'd probably get along well with Tresa Clunard of Purity. She believed in strength through discipline, too.* But aloud he merely said, "The change would really have hurt poor Beti. You tried to change her from alive to dead."

"Beti has the same streak of romanticism you do. I merely wanted to have her brought back here where I could keep an eye on her, to keep her from hurting herself and others." He gave a wry smile and shook his head. "Poor Pias, trying to be a knight coming to the rescue, just like in all those old stories you liked to read. My people had you pegged from the moment you entered Garridan; when you applied for the citizen's card, your fingerprints and retinal patterns were examined and matched up with the old ones we had on file. We knew exactly where you were and what you were doing every step of the way. We wanted to keep you out of trouble, but it seems you have this knack for going where you don't belong."

"And now I suppose you're going to lock me up for my own good, just like you've done with the rest of the family."

Tas didn't get a chance to answer, for at that moment an explosion rocked the walls of the computer facility. It was far enough away to sound merely like a dull roar, but it was quickly followed by two more blasts that came progressively closer.

"What . . . ?" Tas exclaimed as he looked around in confusion. The guards behind him were no less confused, and several of them ran out of the room to investigate this new threat to the computer complex.

Recovering quickly from his moment of astonishment, Tas turned back toward his brother—but Pias was no longer the obliging target. He didn't know, either, what the cause of the explosions was, but he'd

47

been primed to take advantage of any break that might come his way, and when the blasts occurred he was ready to act.

Dropping rapidly behind the desk he'd been searching, he took himself out of Tas's direct line of fire. At the same time he pulled his own blaster from its holster and prepared to fire back. He might never have a better opportunity to fight back against his mad brother, and he was determined to put up the best struggle he could. His native world depended on it.

He did not want to commit fratricide, though, if he could help it, so his first shot was a warning just slightly over his brother's head. Tas Bavol drew back quickly, fired a blast of his own into the desk, and left the room in a hurry. Pias heard him tell the guards to kill the intruder, but Tas himself was not going to wait around to watch the outcome. He had more important things to do—like saving his own hide.

For the next few minutes Pias was too involved in his shootout with the brassies to pay much attention to anything else happening around him. He noted almost as an incidental fact that three more explosions occurred within the computer complex, but none came near enough to distract him from his business.

He wounded two of the security agents before the rest decided to withdraw from the battle. Finally, when the shooting had stopped, he made his way cautiously out of the office, blaster ever at the ready in case of new trouble. The air smelled heavily of ozone but the outer office and the corridor beyond were completely deserted.

Wandering closer to the main hallway, he could see that the civilian personnel at the facility were in a panic over the bombings. They were rushing for the exits, which only made the job of the security guards that much harder. They were trying to deal with sabotage from an unknown source while simultaneously fighting back the tide of humanity surging for the doors.

In the noise and chaos they scarcely noticed Pias in his stolen guard's uniform. He fought his way across the corridor and into the relatively uncrowded side hall-ways, hoping he could get out of here safely with the in-formation he'd learned. He also hoped that somewhere in this incredible labyrinth he might encounter his brother again. Wherever he went, Tas would not fight the crowds at the normal exits; he'd have a special escape route of his own, and Pias wanted to find it.

But it was Tas who found him. Pias was crossing an-other corridor when a blasterbolt sizzled the air just past his head. Pias dived for cover and fired a shot back at his attacker. Tas fled further down the corridor, and Pias scrambled to his feet and ran after him.

The corridor opened into a large rectangular cham-ber, two stories tall and dozens of meters wide on each side. The chamber floor was covered with many of the large tapered pylons that were the latest design in com-puter memory banks. Pias hesitated as he crossed the threshold. The room appeared empty, but his brother could easily be lurking in ambush behind one of the pylons, waiting for him to make a careless move.

Gun at the ready, Pias made quick, darting motions between the pylons, playing a deadly game of hopscotch as he made his way through the chamber. The sounds of the panicky crowd were far away, and the only real noise in the room was a slight electrical buzz that filled the air. The place smelled of starched efficiency and mathematical disinterest. Even though the atmosphere was cool, Pias was beginning to sweat—and he could almost feel his brother doing the same. The game of hide-and-seek continued.

"Pias! Behind you!" yelled a female voice.

Pias whirled, gun at the ready, and spotted the figure of Tas aiming directly at him. He crouched and fired. Tas's shot went barely over his head, but his own aim was truer—he hit Tas in the right leg and the younger man fell to the ground, howling in pain.

"Vonnie!" Pias called. "You're supposed to be waiting at home!"

Yvonne d'Alembert came cautiously out of hiding, a stun-gun in one hand and a blaster in the other. "You

can't expect me to let you have all the fun, can you?"
she said with a smile and a shrug. "Besides, you needed
my help to bail you out."

"I had the situation well in hand, thank you," Pias
said. "But as long as you're here I'll put you to work
helping me wrap up this case."

Pias walked over to where his brother had fallen and
stood over him scornfully. Tas Bavol was cringing in
pain and fear. "You're not going to kill your own
brother, are you?" Tas whimpered piteously.

"Not everyone plays by your twisted rules," Pias
said. "But I can't guarantee what the Empress's reaction will be when she hears what you've been up to.
She's not as sentimental as I am."

He grabbed Tas by the front of his tunic and pulled
him awkwardly to his feet. The younger man howled
from pain.

"But before your case comes to any imperial court,"
Pias continued sternly, "you've got a couple of other
obligations. First, you're going to come with my friend
and me and help us get safely out of this building. Then
you're going to ask the *kriss* to reconvene. There's a
little matter of justice that's been long overdue."

Pias nervously wiped the sweat from his palms. Vonnie continued to hold Tas prisoner downstairs in the
Bavol family's formal meeting room where the *kriss* was
due to convene in another hour or so. But it wasn't the
kriss that made Pias nervous; that was important, to be
sure, but whatever the outcome, he'd already proved he
could make a decent life for himself elsewhere. The confrontation that was to come now, though, was an emotional one that could affect the rest of his life, and
Pias's insides were knotted up. He'd rather be facing a
roomful of enemy blasters than the ordeal before him.

He took a deep breath, let it out slowly, and followed
the nurse into his father's bedroom. The room was kept
dark because mottle fever made its victims' eyes
ultrasensitive to light. Pias paused on the threshold to
accommodate himself to the low illumination.

The room seemed at first unchanged since Pias's last,

unhappy visit to it. The hard slate floor was covered with handwoven rugs, and the majestic ebonwood bureau with its mirror in the carved frame still stood imposingly against the north wall. The massive canopied bed faced the door as regally as ever. Only as Pias's eyes roamed the room did he notice one tiny but significant detail that was different.

The portrait of his late mother still dominated the south wall, surrounded by pictures of the five Bavol children—no, four. One of the pictures had been removed—Pias's. No attempt had been made to rearrange the other portraits into a new symmetry; the missing picture thus made a statement of sorts by its very absence, unbalancing the visual unity of the display.

Duke Kistur Bavol himself was almost lost in the heavy pile of pillows and bedcovers. He had always been a robust, energetic man until Pias had left Newforest the first time to seek the man who'd murdered his fiancée. The last time Pias had seen his father he was sickly, already well consumed by the mottle fever and looking every year of his age.

Now, in his late sixties, the duke was a gaunt parody of a human figure. Most of his hair was gone except for a few frazzled white strands here and there. His skin was drawn tight across his face, giving him a skull-like appearance, and his eyes were dark and sunken in his cheeks. The dark splotches in his complexion that gave his illness its name almost covered all of his body that was visible.

Pias dismissed the nurse with a gesture and took a step forward. The duke asked, "Who . . . ?" in a shaky voice that was barely audible.

"It's Pias, Poppa."

Despite his weakness, Duke Kistur tried to sit up to look at him; then, suddenly remembering that Pias had been disowned, he lay back down and turned over on his side, facing away from the door. He was prepared to ignore his son's existence, no matter how much it hurt him.

Pias, though, was not going to give his father such an easy way out. Walking over to the bed, he sat down beside his father and said, "I'm going to take shameless advantage of the fact that you're an invalid and can't walk away from me. I know my being here is causing you pain because you're supposed to ignore me like the *kriss* said you should. Well, it's causing me pain to be here, too, but I love you, Father, and I'm not going to let it go that easily. You can try not to listen, but you'll have to hear what I say. Then you can make up your mind about me and I'll abide by whatever decision you choose because I'm a good and obedient son. I wasn't able to tell you everything last time I was here. Now I can tell you the story and I hope you'll approve."

With that as prelude he began his story. He told his father that he'd been recruited into the Service of the Empire as a secret agent while he was away from New-forest, and that Yvette, the woman he loved and had married, was also an agent. He'd wanted to tell his father this the last time he'd come home, but Tas had been in the room and Pias didn't trust him. Confirming his worst fears, Tas had muddied the waters and made it look as though Pias were deserting his own people, eventually stirring up enough animosity to have Pias exiled by the *kriss*.

Pias told his father the story of his exploits since leaving Newforest, and of how he'd managed to save the Empire during the Coronation Day Incursion by being unable to pilot a spaceship. He described the beautiful little granddaughter he'd produced and how he'd named her after his mother. And most of all, Pias told him that he'd never turned his back on his people—but that the values he'd been raised with in this very house compelled him to a larger duty toward the Empire as a whole.

"That's all I can say, Father," he concluded. "I know my silence hurt you, and it has hurt me not to be able to tell you. But I was right not to trust Tas. I hope you'll be able to forgive me—and if you can't accept my choices, at least you'll understand that I made them because you brought me up to care about people."

He stopped abruptly as further words refused to come. He looked down at his father's still form. Kistur

Bavol lay silently, with only the slightest breathing to indicate he was alive—but Pias could see in the bureau mirror that his eyes were open and he'd heard every word his son had spoken. Pias waited, scarcely daring to breathe himself, wondering whether paternal love would overcome his father's enormous pride and stubbornness.

After a couple of minutes, when there was no response, Pias stood up and turned sadly to leave the room. If he couldn't convince his own father, he knew he'd stand no chance to reverse the edict of the *kriss*. But at least with Tas certain to be convicted of treason, the family title would pass to Fenelia, his oldest sister. She was a hard-nosed boor and her husband was a lout, but at least they were honest and would not bring disaster to the planet the way Tas had.

"Pias." The duke spoke the name weakly. He turned slightly in the bed and raised his left hand feebly just a few centimeters—but even that tiny sign was enough.

Pias was at his father's side in an instant, putting his arms around the frail body and holding tight. The two men wept openly and unashamed for several minutes, and by the time Pias left the room they were fully reconciled.

Pias walked out of his father's bedroom feeling as though he were on a world of only one-fourth gee, so much weight had been taken from his soul. Let the *kriss* do what it wanted now; he'd won the true battle. His father had accepted him again, and the universe was no longer such an empty place.

As he was about to descend the stairs to ground level, a woman called his name. He turned and felt a sudden chill as he found himself facing Gitana Bavol, his brother's wife. Gitana had long ago been his lover, until he fell in love with her ill-fated sister Miri, and then met Yvette while on his quest for Miri's killer. Gitana could still twist knives of guilt within his soul, even though his passion for her had died long ago.

The intervening years hadn't been as kind to Gitana as they'd been to him. There were tiny age lines at the corners of her eyes and the beginnings of a double chin.

Her waist-length black hair showed wisps of gray, and her always sumptuous figure was considerably plumper than Pias remembered it.

"Hello, Gitana," he said, careful to keep his voice neutral.

"How . . . how are you?"

"Fine, thank you."

"You're on your way to the *kriss* now, aren't you?"

"Yes, and I don't want to be late."

He turned to go, but Gitana grabbed him tightly by the sleeve and refused to let go. "Pias, wait. I . . . You know I'm a proud woman, but you've always been able to make me beg. I'm begging you now, Pias. Please be merciful at the *kriss*."

"Tas will have to stand or fall by his own actions."

"Oh, hang him! I don't care what happens to him—I only married him because you spurned me for that . . . that other woman. But don't make them do anything to me. If there's any trace of the love you once said you felt for me, don't make them exile me. I couldn't take that."

The tension in Pias released so suddenly he almost burst out laughing. How totally characteristic of Gitana —selfish to the end. Beti had told him about some of Gitana's excesses as Marchioness of Newforest, lording it over everyone else and callously ignoring the feelings of those she deemed below her. But there was no evidence she'd engaged in treasonous activities; her worst misfortune was that she'd married a man who had allowed her to indulge her casual cruelties.

"I'll do what I can," he told her. "They'll probably let you divorce Tas and give back a lot of the jewelry I hear you accumulated." With Gitana's father being one of the most influential marquises on Newforest, her sentence was unlikely to be stronger than that.

"Thank you." She looked into his eyes and made it clear she wanted to kiss him, but Pias simply nodded, pulled away from her, and went downstairs to the formal meeting room where the *kriss* would convene.

Pias walked into the chamber with an air of confidence he'd lacked the last time—because now he knew he held the right cards. Many of the planetary nobles had suffered under Tas's regime, seeing their power usurped and their rights reduced. They realized they'd made a mistake sending Pias away, and were looking for a chance to rectify it.

The first part of the session was the trickiest, since the *kriss*, by its own edict, was supposed to ignore Pias's presence. Pias used his newly established legal identity as Gari Nav to argue the case for Pias Bavol, and the members of the convocation were willing to accept the legal fiction temporarily—if only to strike back at Tas Bavol.

Pias argued that at his previous trial he'd been accused of disloyalty to his people by wanting to marry an outsider and leave the planet without giving an adequate explanation. He said that he still could not explain his reasons to the general body of the *kriss*, but that he'd told them to his father and the duke had accepted them as valid. As proof, they established a vidicom link with the master bedroom upstairs, and Duke Kistur confirmed that Pias had explained the situation to his satisfaction, and he no longer believed the charges made against his son.

With the duke's testimony and the knowledge of how badly things had gone because of their previous edict, the members of the *kriss* voted overwhelmingly to rescind the prior decree. Pias Bavol was now officially alive and a member in good standing of the ducal family. His title, Marquis of Newforest, was returned to him and he was restored to his position as heir to the planet upon his father's death. Coming after the reconciliation with his father it felt almost anticlimactic, but Pias cherished the warm feeling nonetheless.

With that matter out of the way, the *kriss* turned to Tas and his crimes against his people. The *kriss*, a throwback to the tribal law from the days before Newforest joined the Empire, held the power of life and death within Newforest society. The majority of the council was at first inclined to condemn Tas to death for his harsh rule over the world. Pias found it ironic and not a little cowardly that these men who sat by while Tas was in power, afraid to challenge him, were ready to speak out boldly against him now that he'd fallen.

Pias ended up arguing in defense of his brother. He told the *kriss* that Tas's major crimes were against the Empire and he should be tried in imperial court where justice would be a little more impartial, but no less stern. The *kriss* next wanted to banish Tas the way they'd banished Pias before, and Pias dissuaded them from that course, too. As far as he was concerned, such ostracism was a cruel abuse of social power, and he secretly vowed that as duke he would end the *kriss*'s right to invoke it.

The subject of Gitana came up only in passing, as her father, sitting in on the *kriss*, asked what would become of her. It was decided that she should divorce Tas, give back much of the wealth she'd coerced from other people while in her position of power, and be severely censured for her activities. Pias thought she was getting off more lightly than she deserved, but he knew she'd be a marked woman from now on and few decent people would associate with her. For a woman as vain as Gitana, that in itself would be a harsh punishment.

Pias left the *kriss* in utter triumph. He'd arrived on Newforest in secret, cast out by family and friends alike and hunted by the authorities. He was now prepared to leave it reconciled to his father, family, and friends, with his titles restored and his brother facing imperial charges for his treasonous acts. The turnaround was so complete that Pias had trouble believing it.

That night, he and his old friend Yuri—a servant in the Bavol household since before Pias was born, and the man who'd helped Beti escape—sat up until dawn, celebrating, drinking sparkling water, and telling jokes and reminiscing.

CHAPTER 6

Brainstorm

With the full authority of the *kriss*, Tas Bavol was
locked up in the jail he himself had built, and his special
police units were disbanded. There were a few touchy
moments when it looked as though the armed security
forces might revolt and try a takeover of the planet.
They were certainly in a good position to do so, but they
thought better of it. After all, they'd only been hired by
Tas Bavol to do a job and were not being charged with
any crimes themselves—except for a few who were part
of Tas's inner circle and knew about the murders of opposition figures. If the police fought against the legal
orders of the *kriss*—and particularly if they took control
of the planet—they would face the retribution of the
Empire and the charge of treason. Their loyalty to Tas
was not that strong, so they grumbled but surrendered
their weapons peacefully.

Since Vonnie was unknown on Newforest, she could
represent SOTE without blowing her cover identity, and
she interrogated Tas Bavol extensively about his role
within the conspiracy. She learned surprisingly little.
Tas had been approached by representatives of the con-

spiracy within a year after Pias's exile. Their offers of increased power were very seductive, and he had agreed to join forces with them. They had laid down the guidelines for consolidating his power on Newforest with a computerized regime, but it was Tas's own enthusiasm for the task that had produced such brutal excesses.

Tas knew little about the hierarchy above him. His orders had come via teletype from the mysterious C. When Tas had expressed to C his concern that SOTE might interfere with his work on Newforest, C had told him not to worry, that such details were covered on another level that was none of Tas's business. C had given Tas so much useful advice—as well as people and equipment—that Tas accepted his subordinate role in the organization.

When his sister Beti escaped, Tas had informed C, who again told him not to worry, that she would be dealt with. Tas had assumed she would be captured and returned to Newforest—but the idea of her near death didn't fill him with fraternal grief.

Under hard questioning, Tas implicated several of his subordinates in the murders of people who'd opposed his rule. A few of them managed to escape, but most were caught in a quick sweep of police action. Tas Bavol and his gang would not terrorize Newforest any longer.

With Tas out of the picture it was time to check out the local SOTE office that should have been warning Headquarters on Earth about the dangerous situation building here on Newforest. It was Vonnie who drew this assignment, too. Now that Pias's banishment was rescinded he was out of disguise, and his face was too well known on Newforest; his cover would be completely blown if he walked into the SOTE office and identified himself as Agent Peacock.

Instead it was Vonnie, unknown on this world, who walked into the SOTE office and flashed her ID as Agent Hedgehog, one of the prime operatives in SOTE's task force. She was escorted immediately into the office of Captain Lafleur, the DesPlainian who'd been put in charge of SOTE on this high-gee world.

"You must be part of the operation that finally crushed Tas Bavol's death squad," Lafleur said before Vonnie even had a chance to explain her business. "Frankly, it's about time. I've been reporting for years on the dangerous buildup going on here, and all I've gotten from Headquarters is silence."

This was a surprise, since Helena had told her that Headquarters had received no alarming reports from Newforest. Vonnie kept her emotions well hidden, however, and simply said, "May I see your copies of those reports, please?"

"Certainly." Captain Lafleur was more than flattered to cooperate with one of the most famous field agents in the Service, and asked his computer to retrieve the appropriate files. Through some programming mix-up the computer was unable to locate those reports, but the thorough Captain Lafleur also had printout copies available for Vonnie's inspection. As he'd said, the reports for the last few years showed his repeated warnings that something untoward was happening on Newforest, and his repeated requests for official action.

Vonnie's anger was somewhat mollified, though there was still the possibility that Lafleur could have faked these reports the instant he'd heard about Tas Bavol's capture. She asked him to make extra copies of the reports for her and, while he was busy doing so, she made a confidential subcom call to Helena von Wilmenhorst back on Earth.

She found Helena in a jubilant mood. The forces of the Empire had just defeated the conspiracy's ambush plans and routed the enemy ships. The supposed alien invaders were merely a hoax dreamed up by the conspiracy, and were no additional threat at all. Jules, Yvette, and Captain Paul Fortier, who had gone on the secret mission to Omicron, had all returned safely—and to top it all off, Lady A, the apparent leader of the conspiracy, had been killed during the long space battle. The entire Service was rejoicing at its triumph. Helena told Vonnie that Jules had hurt his leg during the mis-

59

sion, but was recovering nicely.

Vonnie, too, rejoiced—primarily at the news that her husband had survived such a deadly ambush. After giving vent to momentary elation, she became serious again and gave a verbal report on the recent events on Newforest. She closed by explaining the mystery of Captain Lafleur's reports. If they were genuine, they let the local SOTE office off the hook—but that would raise the new specter that someone in SOTE Headquarters itself was collaborating with the conspiracy. The Service had known for some time that information of the highest secrecy was available to the conspiracy—but there was a significant difference between a leak and a mole within SOTE actively sabotaging the Service's operations. Helena promised to investigate the reports from Newforest to see where the communications breakdown had occurred.

Vonnie left Tas Bavol's care to Captain Lafleur. She knew this was a risk; if Lafleur really was tied in with the conspiracy it would give him and Tas a chance to escape together. But it would also be a chance for him to prove his loyalty to the Service anew. Since Tas Bavol had been stripped of his power and was no longer of great value to the conspiracy, the risk would be a minimal one. Helena would be sending an investigative team to Newforest as standard operating procedure, so Captain Lafleur couldn't do much damage even if he did defect.

Vonnie and Pias stayed on Newforest another week while the ship Pias had come in was rescued from the forest and restored to its original condition. Pias called Beti back on DesPlaines to tell her the good news that she was no longer an exile. He rebuilt ties to his family and friends, though many of his acquaintances felt so guilty about what they'd done to him that the relationships could never be fully restored. Pias also spent time reestablishing himself as heir to the planet and dismantling the evil bureaucracy that his brother had built in the name of efficiency. The jails were emptied of their political prisoners and Tas's accomplices took their place. As heir to the planet, Pias formally requested that SOTE establish a temporary administrative regime until a final decision could be made on his future role.

Vonnie stayed in a hotel room in Garridan, keeping away from Pias as much as possible. The less they were seen together, the better it would be for their cover identities as SOTE agents. Vonnie became an ordinary tourist, visiting shops and places of interest and buying little presents for Jules, Maurice, and other people she cared about.

Finally, with the ship repaired, Pias's departure could be delayed no longer. The farewell to his family—and particularly to his father—was tearful and sad, but this time Pias could promise he'd return frequently to visit and keep in touch with what was happening on his native world—and he'd also keep close contact with SOTE to be sure Newforest had the kind of government it deserved. He also promised to bring Yvette and little Kari back for a visit at the earliest opportunity, to allow grandfather and granddaughter a chance to see one another.

With Vonnie aboard, Pias lifted his ship off Newforest and set a course back to DesPlaines. Once they were safely in subspace, he and Yvonne had their first real chance for a conversation without having to censor everything they said for security purposes. "Just how did you manage to be in the right place at the right time?" Pias wondered.

His sister-in-law smiled. "Thinking over what you said back on DesPlaines, I realized you were probably right—I'd stick out horribly as an outsider in Newforest society. So I decided to go there and be an official outsider—I booked passage on commercial spaceliners and arrived as a tourist. It gave me more freedom than you had. I was able to smuggle some weapons and explosives in my luggage, and I wasn't given a citizen's card so I never got hassled. Apparently they wanted to be careful about playing games like that on outsiders who might go home and talk about it to the wrong people. As a plain old tourist from DesPlaines I could walk around un-

61

disturbed and do things a citizen would never be allowed to do.

"I got here, I think, about three days after you did. Garridan's such a small town that it wasn't hard for me to find you and keep an eye on you. After a while I noticed the police watching you, too. It was very subtle; with that citizen's card to keep track of your movements they didn't need heavy surveillance. I barely noticed it myself, so I'm not surprised you didn't see it. I saw you steal that guard's uniform and go into the computer complex. A couple of minutes later a whole platoon of guards went in after you, so I decided it was time for me to step in. I threw a few grenades to distract the guards at the gate long enough for me to get inside and I tried to keep the chaos going to help you if you needed it—which you did."

Pias smiled. "I can't exactly say I'm glad you ignored my advice, but I am pleased with the results. I'm just glad I'm not Jules. Eve is headstrong enough for me to deal with; I'll let *him* try to argue you down in the future."

A pleasant surprise awaited them as their ship landed at Felicité's private spacefield. Yvette had caught a fast ship in from Earth and was there to provide them with a hero's welcome. Pias spotted her the instant he left the airlock, and he raced down the boarding ramp and across the field to take her in his arms. They'd been apart the last few weeks, with Yvette on an assignment so dangerous there'd been a good chance she'd never return. Even though he'd heard from Vonnie that the mission was successful, this was the first opportunity he'd had to let out the tensions he'd felt. Now he grabbed Yvette, kissed her, and held her so tightly that if she were any less strong a woman she'd have snapped in two.

"I was so worried about you," he told her when he finally stopped kissing her long enough to speak. "It was hell to have you so far away and in so much danger, and not be able to do anything to help you. I hope we never have to go through that again.''

"I do, too," Yvette said, and there were tears of happiness in her eyes. "And Helena told me a little bit of what you were up to on Newforest. I'm so happy for you, to be back in with your family again; I know how much it would hurt if my family turned against me. I love you, Pias, and I'm glad your family can show their love again.''

Pias nodded. "It's no fun having a traitor for a brother, and some of the rest of them are rather forgettable—but yes, I'm glad I've got them, too.''

He and Yvette finally separated from their embrace and noticed, as though for the first time, that Vonnie was standing patiently beside them with a small smile on her face. Yvette returned the smile and reached out to take her sister-in-law's hand. "Hello, Vonnie," she said. "I'm sorry Jules isn't here for you. He had to go back to Nereid to pick up the *Comet*; can't just leave it sitting around some strange spaceport when we might need it at any moment. He promised to come straight back after he picked it up.''

Vonnie squeezed Yvette's hand reassuringly and said, "That's smooth. As long as I know he survived I'm not worried.''

Yvette hesitated, then decided to let Jules tell her about the severity of his injury. While there was no doubt at all that Jules would recover, he would never again have quite the same agility or lightning responses that had made him one of the handful of people ever to get a perfect score on the Service's Thousand Point Test. His mind was undiminished and his body would still put normal men to shame—but his days as SOTE's top agent were definitely numbered.

The trio drove back to Felicité and Pias quickly made a call to the Roumenier manor where his sister was staying, telling her she'd be receiving an imperial commendation for her bravery in bringing the Newforest problem to official attention. Her greatest delight was that Pias's name had been restored and he was officially a member of her family again. "I never wanted to lose you, Pias," she said. "You were everything a big brother should be, and I'm glad to have you back again."

When Pias told her she was free to go home whenever she wanted, however, she hesitated. Puzzled, Pias pressed her and finally got the admission that she'd been seeing a lot of Vonnie's brother, Jacques Roumenier, and was quite taken with him. They'd been doing a lot of sightseeing around DesPlaines, and Beti wasn't sure she wanted to go home just yet. Pias admitted she couldn't be *compelled* to go back to Newforest, and wished her happy hunting. He was smiling broadly as he blew her a kiss goodbye and broke the vidiphone connection.

Just before dinnertime a subcom call came in from Helena von Wilmenhorst to let them know how the situation stood at Headquarters. Since Vonnie's last report from Newforest, a systematic investigation of SOTE's files had been conducted and the reports from Captain Lafleur were found. Somehow, in a way no one could understand, those reports had all been misclassified and misfiled so that the information they contained had never reached the proper people. This gave the false impression that everything had been smooth on Newforest when in fact the situation was quite different.

"There's a pattern to this that Father doesn't like at all," Helena said. "As he points out, once can be an accident, twice is a coincidence, and three or more times is enemy action. Three years' worth of reports don't get misfiled by mistake. Someone made a deliberate effort to close our eyes to a deteriorating situation—which is exactly what happened to us on the Banion case. It makes us wonder exactly how many other reports have been similarly misrouted, falsified, or destroyed. We're going to have to conduct a thorough survey of everything we've got—and try to do it quietly so we don't alarm the conspiracy.

"I don't mind telling you that Father and I are just plain scared. If this sort of thing is widespread, it could make the Banion affair look like a tea party. We're going to do some more preliminary work before we turn you loose on the case, and we'll keep you informed as soon as we find anything. Keep your fingers crossed, and keep hoping that Newforest was an anomaly, an isolated incident. But be ready to move at any second.''

Yvette felt a chill go down her spine. Pias had not been involved in the Banion matter and Vonnie had only been in it peripherally, but it had been one of the most horrifying chapters in SOTE's long history. Banion the Bastard had managed to infiltrate his people into every level of the Service, and weeding them out had been an excruciatingly painful process. Now, despite the most rigorous loyalty tests anyone could have devised, it looked as though that process would have to be repeated.

Helena closed the call on a more upbeat note, informing Pias and Vonnie of what Yvette already knew: that Helena had become engaged to Captain Paul Fortier of Naval Intelligence. Vonnie had never met him and Pias had met only his treacherous robot double, but both had heard stories of the man's exploits. He'd saved Yvette's life on the pirate base just before the Coronation Day Incursion, and he'd helped Helena and the Circus track down the identity of Lady A. He had just returned from the dangerous mission to Omicron with Jules and Yvette, and was an outstanding security agent. Pias and Vonnie congratulated Helena on her good fortune and wished her every success in the future.

Helena's report cast a slight pall over the dinner that evening as the import of what it could mean for all of them began to sink in. However, as Yvette began relating her adventures working with Lady A against the ''alien invaders'' of Omicron, everyone's spirits picked up; a rousing adventure yarn with a happy ending always made them feel better. Vonnie and Pias, as others had done before them, puzzled over the meaning of Lady A's defiant final words that the conspiracy *was* the Empire and that SOTE would have to destroy the Empire in order to save it. They could not solve the riddle there at the dinner table, however, so instead Pias and Vonnie told Yvette about their own adventures on Newforest.

''In a way, Newforest just fought off its own alien invasion," Pias observed to his wife. "All that computerized equipment and jackboot efficiency are totally foreign to the Newforest way of doing things. We've always prided ourselves on being an easygoing people with a great disdain for rules and regulations imposed on us from the outside. No wonder Tas ended up being so thoroughly hated by everyone on the planet."

"That's the way the conspiracy's always been," Vonnie said. "Ruthless, cold, and efficient. Look at its leader, Aimée Amorat—a heartless woman to begin with, put into a mechanical body with all the soul of a polished brass doorknob. You were there when she cold-bloodedly killed her own granddaughter in an effort to get at you. The conspiracy treats people no better than machines. Even if I didn't like Edna I'd still rather see her on the throne than anyone the conspiracy would put there."

The glimmer of an idea flashed through Yvette's mind, and then was gone again before she could identify it. She tried to reach in and recover it, but it remained tantalizingly out of her grasp and eventually she gave up the effort. She returned her attention to the dinner table conversation, which had strayed onto the subject of Helena's engagement to Captain Fortier.

That night, Yvette had a dream. She and Pias were on Newforest facing Tas Bavol, who was now a giant towering above their heads and threatening to squash them with his boot. They ran into a forest of shiny aluminum trees as Tas's laughter followed them—only now it wasn't Tas, but the even more dangerous Lady A, her coldly beautiful features staring down at them from an enormous computer screen suspended above their heads. The trees slowly merged into towering cones of computer banks, and an army of faceless robots moved in from all sides, firing blasters at the two SOTE agents. No matter where they ran, that face on the computer screen stared down at them, watching, watching. . . .

Yvette sat bolt upright in bed, her body clammy with sweat. Her eyes were wide open, staring into the dark-

66

ness of the room before her, focusing on nothing and yet seeing something far greater than she'd ever seen before.

"Mon Dieu!" she whispered, and her whole body began to tremble with the enormity of her vision.

Beside her in the bed, Pias came instantly awake. Her reaction was so severe that at first he looked around for some physical threat—but all was quiet in Felicité. But something was definitely wrong; Yvette was a woman without fear, and Pias had never seen her act this way before.

"Eve? What's the matter?" he asked, sitting up beside her and putting his arms around her naked shoulders. Her skin felt as cold as a corpse.

"Mon Dieu!" Yvette repeated through her shivers.

"Tell me what the matter is," Pias insisted.

Yvette blinked and looked around, as though realizing for the first time where she was. She turned her head fearfully, as though expecting to see goblins in every corner. "I can't," she said softly. "I don't know where they are. They could be anywhere, listening, watching. They'll kill me, they'll kill you if they knew I know. They can do it, Pias, more easily than you can swat a buzzfly." Her trembling increased.

This behavior was totally uncharacteristic of the woman he knew and loved, but Pias was determined to solve the mystery. "Is there anything I can do?" he asked.

"Hold me. Tightly."

That, at least, was an easy and pleasant task. He held her body tightly against his own, while Yvette went through a shivering fit that rocked the entire bed. "This is bigger and deeper than anyone ever suspected," she whispered in her husband's ear. "She was right, it will destroy the whole Empire. But we can't let it succeed, no matter what the cost. We have to stop it."

The shivering fit stopped abruptly as Yvette worked through her moment of panic. Her muscles relaxed and she became abnormally calm; her respiration returned to its usual rate and her hands were steady. Pias had seen this mood overtake her before, a cold, detached fury, and he pitied anything on which Yvette turned that anger.

"I'm smooth now," she said calmly as she pulled herself away from him. "Thank you for holding me. I needed it. I know what we have to do now."

"Well, would you mind telling me?"

Yvette rolled casually off the bed and strode to the closet. She knew instinctively where everything was, and began assembling her wardrobe in the dark. "We are going to get dressed this minute—you, me, and Vonnie if she can pack fast enough—and we're going down to the spacefield. We're picking the fastest ship available, and you're going to fly us at top speed to Earth. Once we're in subspace I can tell you what I'm thinking, and maybe then you'll tell me I'm crazy and have me committed to an institution for the terminally confused. But if you agree with me. . . ." She stopped and closed her eyes, not wanting to face the possibility.

Pias got out of bed, turned on the light, and began to get dressed himself. Yvette had one of the most brilliantly intuitive minds he'd ever known; she would not become this frightened for no reason. "Anything else?" he asked as he dressed.

"Yes. We're going to pray harder than we've ever prayed in our lives. We're going to pray for two things. First, we're going to pray that I'm totally, completely, dead wrong. Second, if I'm not, we're going to pray that we're not too late to save at least some tatters of the Empire before it all collapses in a heap around us!"

CHAPTER 7

A Somber Picnic

Being Head of the Service of the Empire was never an easy task, and it seemed to be getting harder these days. The hours were always long, the work went largely unrecognized, and if the job was done properly no one would realize you'd ever done anything. When the Service was working at peak efficiency, there never appeared to be a need for its services.

These days, though, the job seemed tougher than usual. The Service had barely had time to rejoice over its triumph at saving the Navy from a disastrous ambush in the "Gastaadi War"—a disaster averted by only the slimmest of margins—when it was faced with the discovery, based on the Newforest situation, that its intelligence evaluation system had been sabotaged. How many other planetary files had been concealed or altered, leading SOTE to think the situation within the Empire was smoother than it really was? Were there planets in worse shape than Newforest, securely under the enemy's domination while the Empire did nothing? Who was committing this sabotage? How was it accomplished? And, above all, how could it be combatted?

69

Grand Duke Zander von Wilmenhorst and his daughter Helena puzzled over these problems for days. It was an ironic twist of fate that the very urgency of these matters compelled them to move slowly. They'd known for years that the conspiracy was aware of nearly every move they made, but they'd never been able to seal the leak. If they suddenly began a massive search through the files, it would tip off the enemy that the Service knew something was amiss. That, in turn, might lead the conspiracy to take some precipitate action, and no one knew in what direction the currently wounded enemy would jump.

The Head agonized for some time over how to disguise what he was doing, and eventually hit upon a plan. He would announce an efficiency incentive drive within the Service; those officers and branches with the best records would receive bonuses and promotions. Naturally, to evaluate performance accurately, all past records had to be checked and files had to be reread. A handful of his most trusted aides were given the task of sorting through all the records, and only they were told what they were *really* looking for—files that had been deliberately misplaced or falsified to give the impression that conditions were better than they really were. With more than thirteen hundred planets in the Empire, the task was laborious and time-consuming—but it was utterly essential if a true picture of the state of the Empire was to emerge.

This effort was just beginning, and the Head was trying to make everything appear perfectly normal, when he suddenly got a call from Yvette Bavol on his personal comline. The fact that the call didn't come over the subcom meant that Yvette was back here on Earth, which surprised him; normally she would have told him she was coming first. That put him instantly on the alert.

"Well, sir, I'm back, just as you requested," Yvette smiled at him over the vidicom screen.

He had requested no such thing, and they both knew it. "Yes, thank you for being so prompt." He had no idea what the matter was, but he would play the game by her rules until he found out. He knew enough to trust the d'Alembert instincts.

"Is today a good day for that picnic at the beach you and Helena promised me? I remember you telling me about that one deserted stretch where nobody ever goes."

"It may be difficult for us to get away from the office today. . . ."

"I realize you're a busy man and other things may take priority, but I can think of ten good reasons why you should come on this picnic."

"Ten?" he asked.

"At least," Yvette said solemnly. "Maybe even more."

The Head was stunned. A Priority Ten situation, to which Yvette was obviously alluding, referred to an imminent invasion or armed rebellion. It was the highest priority rating an emergency could have—yet Yvette was saying this one could rank even higher.

What made things even worse was the method Yvette was using to report this to him. She was not going through the proper channels; she was not using a scrambler; she was not using any of SOTE's official codes. To the Head, that could only mean one thing: Yvette felt the Service had been so compromised that all of its official communications, no matter how thickly disguised, were open to enemy inspection. The only method of communication she felt safe with was face to face in some deserted spot where there was no likelihood of their conversation being overheard.

In such matters he trusted the d'Alemberts more thoroughly than anyone else in the Galaxy, even his own daughter. If Yvette Bavol was this alarmed, there had to be a good reason for it—and that deserved his instant and undivided attention.

"Now that you mention it," he said, trying to match her casual tone, "Helena and I have been working awfully hard the last few weeks. A picnic at the beach sounds like a relaxing change of pace." He described a spot along the Florida coastline where he knew they wouldn't be interrupted, and added, "We'll be there in about an hour."

"Better hurry," Yvette said. "I can hardly wait."

The Head broke the connection and buzzed his daughter over the intercom. "Helena," he said, "call down to the commissary and have them pack us a picnic lunch, on the double. We're going to the beach this afternoon."

The weather, at least, was cooperative. A few small white clouds dotted the blue sky and the sun shone pleasantly. The day was warm, though there was enough of a breeze to keep it from being unbearable.

Vonnie d'Alembert and the Bavols arrived in a rented copter half an hour early for the rendezvous. They landed the craft almost half a kilometer from the designated spot, and Pias and Yvette walked in with their picnic basket, looking as innocent as they could be. By prior consent, Vonnie stayed with the copter; she would keep an eye on the proceedings to make sure nothing interfered with the discussion. At the slightest sign of trouble, she was prepared to leap into action to protect her friends and associates.

The Bavols spread a blanket on the warm sand and waited. At the expected time another copter carrying Grand Duke Zander and Duchess Helena flew into sight. It circled for a moment, then landed a few hundred meters away. The Head and his daughter got out and walked casually across the beach to the spot where the Bavols had spread their blanket. While Pias and Yvette were wearing shorts and light shirts, the von Wilmenhorsts were not dressed for the beach. The Head was in one of his standard gray suits and Helena was wearing one of the jumpsuits that were so much her signature style. They'd had no time to change clothes to something more appropriate, so the meeting on the beach was an odd blend of casual and formal.

As her bosses approached, Yvette scanned them with the portable detector she'd brought with her. They were clean; neither had any listening devices planted on their clothing. Both were carrying miniature blasters, but that was only to be expected.

The Head, feeling strange emotional echoes of his shoreline meeting with Lady A just a few weeks earlier, wasted no time with small talk. As soon as he and Helena sat down on the blanket, he asked, "What's the emergency?"

Yvette took a deep breath and let it out slowly. "I think I know who C is," she said, "and if I'm right, the whole Empire is in imminent danger."

"Who?" Helena asked breathlessly.

"Not so fast," Yvette said. "This has to be built up slowly or it'll sound crazy and you'll lock me away. Pias and Vonnie had trouble believing it when I told them. . . ."

"Yet the more we thought about it," Pias interrupted, "the more we realized she's probably right. It's screwy and insane, but it makes so much sense it's scary."

"*Khorosho*," the Head said. "Give it to me at your own speed."

"I got the idea from listening to Pias's story of what happened on Newforest," Yvette began. "He was fascinated at how efficient it all was, and how computerized such a backward planet had become in so short a time. Vonnie pointed out that the entire conspiracy acted with the cold efficiency of a machine.

"Let's examine what we know about C. No one's ever seen him, with the possible exception of Lady A. When Jules and Vonnie questioned her on Gastonia she gave them a description of him, almost certainly false. Later we learned that she told Tanya Boros there was no such person as C. With Aimée, it was always hard to know when she was telling the truth and when she was planting false clues to mislead us. But you said yourself, sir, that the best lies contain an element of truth. Maybe there *is* no such person as C.

"We know that the conspiracy has access to the Empire's innermost secrets. You've tried for years to trace the leaks, without success; no matter what loyalty tests

73

you give, our people keep passing them. Now we've learned that not only does the conspiracy have access to our information, it's actively tampering with it in subtle ways to give us a false sense of security.

"Then there's the question of resources. The conspiracy has built huge fleets of ships and found crews to man them. Some of the income came from piracy, but piracy isn't *that* lucrative. The conspiracy has huge space manufacturing bases and battle stations. Jules and Vonnie smashed the arms manufacturing plant on Slag, but weapons are still coming from somewhere. The conspiracy found an entire planet, Sanctuary, that had somehow been passed over by imperial explorers, and built a civilization on it. They hid from us the fact that traitors were routinely being taken off Gastonia and returned to the ranks of the conspiracy. They were even able to design and build an entire race of alien invaders to lure us into an almost-fatal ambush.

"Hidden resources. A war of information. Machine-like efficiency. The conspiracy's emblem is an integrated circuit chip. And no one's ever seen C; they just get his orders over the teletype."

"You're saying the whole conspiracy works by computers," Helena said. "There's nothing new in that theory. In order to get all the information it knows about us, the conspiracy has to be tapping our files somewhere. But different kinds of information are available in different places, using different codes and different security clearances. No one person, not even Father—not even the Empress unless she really tried—has access to all of it. There'd have to be a widespread coalition of computer operators, a whole army of them, to achieve those results. And if that many computer operators were working against us, our tests should have given us some indication of it by now."

Yvette smiled grimly. "Not an army of computer operators," she said. "The computers themselves."

A silence descended, broken only by the pounding of the waves. At last the Head said, "Explain yourself."

"The Primary Computer Complex processes information from all over the Empire—everything from rainfall statistics on Floreata to actuarial tables for Nevander. The computers at SOTE Headquarters are closely linked to it; so are the computers at Luna Base. Every action the Navy takes, every bit of information the Service gathers, is stored away in the computer system.

"In addition, the computer tells us what course of action to take. We let it correlate the data for us, and then it tells us what to do about it. It may say, 'This situation here looks suspicious; investigate it.' Or it may say, 'Everything's fine over here; don't bother looking any closer.' The computer regulates shipping schedules and interstellar commerce. When credit transfers are made between banks, no real money changes hands; it all goes through the computer and comes out the other side— supposedly unchanged.

"If the PCC is our enemy, then *we* are the leak we've been looking for. The reports we write are given to computer operators who are totally loyal to the Empire, and they program the information into the computer—feeding it straight to our worst enemy without even realizing it. No wonder the conspiracy knew everything we were doing—we were telling them all along, every step of the way. In return, the PCC gave us back the information it *wanted* us to know—and as a result we just stumbled from crisis to crisis, escaping by a narrower and narrower margin each time. We had to run at top speed just to close the gap between what we thought we knew and what was really happening."

"But . . . but the computer's just a machine, a sophisticated calculator," Helena protested. "How can it come alive and plot an entire revolution?"

"The Primary Computer Complex is the most complicated system ever devised," the Head said quietly. "It was designed by the most brilliant team of cyberneticists ever assembled. It's so intricate that even they admitted no one person could ever understand the whole thing. Suppose that somewhere along the line, in the midst of all that complexity, the PCC developed consciousness, an awareness of itself—a mind."

"Exactly," Yvette nodded. "We've seen what the conspiracy can do with artificial intelligence. They made robots that looked and acted so much like people it was impossible to tell without special equipment. The conspiracy knows how to make a machine duplicate human thought. What better explanation than if the leader of the conspiracy were a machine itself?"

" 'A' stood for Amorat, a simple, logical abbreviation," Pias said. "Why shouldn't 'C' stand for Computer? It would explain why we've never found anyone named 'B' in their hierarchy, and why 'A' wasn't necessarily higher in rank."

"But *why*?" Helena persisted. "Why would a machine *want* to take over the Empire?"

"I don't know," Yvette admitted. "As I said, it sounded screwy to me, too. But regardless of why, the more I look at it, the more this theory seems to make sense."

"Why would anyone want to take over the Empire?" the Head asked philosophically. "It's a killer of a job. I've heard Bill and Edna both say, on more than one occasion, how tempting it would be to trade it all in for a simpler life. Maybe it's the fact that *any* life form tries to make order out of its surroundings, to protect itself. The more advanced the life form, the more order it seems to need. If the PCC has become, in some sense, alive, then it might want to control its environment— meaning the Empire. As a very advanced organism, it would need very thorough control."

He fell silent for several minutes, contemplating the situation, and the others respected his silence. "If your hypothesis is correct," he said at last, "you've just handed us a hell of a problem."

"I know," Yvette said quietly. "I still get the shakes thinking about it, I'm so scared."

"Bozhe moi!" Helena gasped suddenly.

"What is it?" Pias asked.

"Something just occurred to me. When I was on Dr. Loxner's asteroid and he was talking about putting

Aimée Amorat into a robot body, he said he tried to talk her into entering a computer the way he did. She told him no—she already had a computer."

"Not just *a* computer," Pias said. "*The* computer."

"It also brings Amorat's final words into perspective," the Head said. "In a very real sense, the PCC is the glue that holds the Empire together. It's the central nervous system of the Galaxy. If we destroy the brain, can the body of the Empire survive?

"The PCC itself controls very little directly. We *thought* it was used mostly for storage and analysis of data. But it has direct link-ups with SOTE's computer facilities and with the Navy's computer array at Luna Base, so we'll have to assume they're an extended part of its system. It also has its own independent subcom network, which means it could be in touch with—and re-program—virtually any computer in the Empire."

"You see now why I'm so scared," Yvette said. "There's hardly an aspect of our lives these days that isn't influenced by computers somehow. If they all went haywire, the Empire would be in chaos within hours."

The Head nodded gravely. " 'Chaos' is a mild way of putting it. The Empire could very easily be destroyed, just as Amorat predicted. Plus there's the fact that the conspiracy's forces are prepared for such a contingency, more than we are; the instant a power vacuum occurs, they'll be all set to march in and take over. We've just scored a decisive victory over their fleet, so we can be grateful we don't have to look at a threat from that direction—but there'll be plenty of other threats to worry about. The big problem, of course, is how we're going to stop the PCC from causing its damage."

"Can't we just turn it off?" Pias asked. "It's only a machine."

"Could you just turn off the FitzHugh and Fortier robots?" Yvette asked him. "They were only machines, too."

"Yvette's right," the Head said. "The Primary Computer Complex may be only a machine, but it's the most intricate machine ever built. You've never been there, you've never seen just how incredible it is. It's got its own power source, its own armaments, its own defense screens, even its own subspace engines in case it's ever attacked and has to escape. We've always known how pivotal the PCC was to the Empire's survival. We knew that if we lost it we'd be in deep trouble, so we made sure it was the most secure place in the entire Galaxy. I can see we're now going to pay dearly for our precautions."

He paused and stared out at the ocean for several seconds. "I'm going to have to give this a lot of thought, and very quickly," he said. "We'll have to act fast, but not precipitously. Edna will have to be notified, of course—in person, since we have to assume the computer is monitoring all communications channels. That'll mean a trip to Moscow for me tonight. She'll have to make the final decision in the matter, and I don't envy her. One way or another, the Empire is in for a major shock—and since she *is* the Empire in a very real sense, this will hit her hard."

The Head looked piercingly at the Bavols. "I'll want the two of you to stay right here on Earth until we know what we're doing. Is Vonnie with you, by any chance?"

"Yes, she's back there by the copter, keeping watch."

"Good. I'm only sorry Jules is way off on Nereid at the moment—but right now, anything suspicious, like calling in my best agent for no apparent reason, might alarm the PCC, and we can't take that risk. I'm glad that at least I have you three here. The Empire is about to go through a firestorm, and I want my finest agents where I can find them at a moment's notice."

CHAPTER 8

Attack on the PCC

Edna Stanley, eleventh ruler in the unbroken dynasty that had reigned since the founding of the Empire of Earth, was not in a very receptive mood. Just two days ago she'd returned to Earth from the far-off planet Omicron, where she'd personally observed the destruction wrought by the conspiracy's fiendish plot, and where she'd promised the inhabitants relief from their misery. Since Omicron was at the farthest limits of the Empire, travel each way was long and, while not arduous, certainly less comfortable than she was used to. Making that journey on such short notice had required a drastic rearrangement of her already busy schedule, and now that she'd returned there were dozens of duties that all required her immediate and simultaneous attention. She was running in circles trying to meet all her obligations—and on top of that, she'd contracted a mild head cold. It was not strong enough to incapacitate her, just bad enough to make her outlook on the world that much more dismal.

As if all that weren't bad enough, along came an unexpected personal visit from Grand Duke Zander von

Wilmenhorst. While she always thought of him as a dear, beloved uncle, she couldn't help also thinking of him as an omen of doom. Their respective schedules were both so crowded that they seldom had time to see one another unless it was on imperial business—and since Zander's business was the security of the Empire, that usually meant something was wrong.

It was most uncharacteristic of the Grand Duke to barge in without calling ahead first. While the Head of the Service of the Empire had unrestricted access to the Empress any time of the day or night, he normally conducted emergency business by vidicom. Edna wondered what problem could have caused this break in the accustomed formality.

She soon found out. Grand Duke Zander passed her a handwritten note suggesting that they go for a walk in the imperial gardens. Even though it was the middle of an autumn morning in Moscow, Edna knew better than to deny the request. She donned a sable cape over her businesswoman's suit-dress to combat the fall chill, and she and her old friend went for an unescorted walk through the elaborate gardens that filled the northwest corner of the palace grounds.

There, amid that gorgeous setting, Zander von Wilmenhorst outlined to her the grave threat that faced the Empire. The Empress listened calmly, as she always did, and sat down on a marble bench to contemplate the problem for several minutes in silence.

At last she spoke. "You haven't a bit of proof for any of these suppositions, do you?" she asked.

"Not a shred," the Grand Duke admitted. "They're based on pure guesswork—but every bit of circumstantial evidence seems to confirm the theory. And the guesswork itself comes from Yvette Bavol; I'd trust her intuitions with my life. I've tried every way I could to punch a hole in her arguments, and they remain airtight.

"This theory accounts for so many things. It explains why a woman as grasping and egocentric as Aimée Amorat would share power with someone else—because even if the computer ended up running things, she would still be the figurehead empress. It explains why the conspiracy relies so much on robots, automated battle stations, and human machines like Lady A and Dr. Loxner, and why it handles the people who work for it with machinelike precision. It explains how the conspiracy was able to tamper with our files, how they were able to finance their operations, and how they could get away with the operations on Gastonia. It explains why they knew virtually everything we were doing and why we could never trace the leaks."

"If the PCC is so all-powerful, why are we still here?" Edna asked. "Surely with the kind of power you describe it should have eliminated us long ago and taken over for itself."

"I'm tempted to say it was luck, though where the d'Alemberts are concerned I think they make their own luck. Remember, that family has always been our secret weapon—so secret that nothing about them as our agents has ever been written down or entered into any files. That's been a big void in the PCC's knowledge of our operations—only the d'Alemberts, when the rest of SOTE was helpless, have managed to save the day. The PCC may have guessed something about the Circus's involvement—it's a simple correlation that the Circus has visited some trouble spots and the trouble suddenly vanished—but it can't really know the extent of that involvement. The PCC tried to lure Jules and Yvette out into the open by using doubles for them, but it knew so little about the true nature of Agents Wombat and Periwinkle that it miscalculated and the trick backfired. It tried to discredit me, but it underestimated the Circus's ability to dig out the truth. If I hadn't appreciated how valuable the d'Alemberts were before, I certainly do now."

"But there's still no proof," Edna said. "The PCC is the single most important tool that holds the Empire together. You're asking me to destroy it on the basis of speculations and unproved theories."

"Ordinarily, as you know, I counsel conservative action. But in this case, where something so monstrous and monumental is concerned, I must urge radical action. I feel like a doctor wanting to amputate a limb in

81

order to save the whole body."

"This isn't a limb, it's the brain itself. If your theory is right, then of course the PCC should be destroyed as quickly as possible no matter what the consequences for the Empire. But if you're wrong, if we destroy the PCC and it doesn't affect the conspiracy, we'll have done their job for them. We'll have destroyed our information system and our ability to coordinate action at various places throughout the Galaxy. We'll be more vulnerable to enemy attack than we ever were before. What would you do then?"

"I'd resign, of course, and take full responsibility for the action—up to and including being executed for treason."

"You're wrong on two counts," Edna said somberly. "The responsibility for the decision is ultimately mine, and I won't use you as a scapegoat. And it's *my* neck on the chopping block more than yours—I'd be dead before I had a chance to sign your execution order." She sighed. "Are you certain that by taking quick action we can at least save the bulk of the Empire?"

"No," the Grand Duke said, and when Edna looked at him questioningly he continued, "Even if we could knock out the PCC with one quick blow before it could order a counterstrike, that doesn't guarantee a thing. It may already have sent out destructive programs to computers throughout the Empire, with itself in an inhibitory position. That would be like a dead man's switch. The destructive programs wouldn't go into effect as long as the PCC was around to tell them no—but the instant the PCC is destroyed, there would be nothing to stop the chaos. That, at least, is the way I'd plan it if I were on the other side."

He looked squarely into the Empress's eyes. "We must face the fact, Your Majesty, that if we take this route, no matter how successful we are, the Empire as we know it is doomed. We can try to salvage some of it, but we can't hope for much and we can't count on any. The PCC has had many years to consider its strategy. I've had less than a day. If I had six months I might think of some way to gently divorce the PCC from control of the Galaxy—but we don't dare wait that long. Sooner or later, through some wrong word or inadvertent slip, the PCC will learn that we know its secret. At that moment it will take its decisive action whether we're ready or not. I'd rather be the one to pick the time. We can't stop the blow that will fall, but at least we can brace ourselves for when it hits."

In all her life, Edna Stanley had never known Grand Duke Zander to make such a gloomy forecast. Certainly he'd given realistic appraisals, but always with the underlying current of optimism that the storm could be weathered. Now even that ray of hope was denied her. There was nothing defeatist or resigned about Zander's expression; he was, and always would be, a fighter for the proper order in the Galaxy. But he was trying to impress on her the realistic assumption that no matter what course they took, there would be substantial losses.

"Very well," Edna said, realizing that the fate of the Empire, of trillions of people, rested on her shoulders. "You've been right so many times before I'll have to trust you this time. We'll go ahead with your plan and hope we can survive the backlash. What do you expect me to do?"

"Other than giving your approval, you do nothing. We don't want to give the PCC the slightest reason to suspect we know about it. I do insist, though, that when we make our move you should be as far away from civilization as you can be. Go rafting down the Grand Canyon, go inspect sand dunes in the Gobi Desert—anywhere away from machines. If I can at least keep you safe, we're halfway back toward rebuilding what's bound to be destroyed."

The Primary Computer Complex was not located on Earth itself. An asteroid twenty-five kilometers in diameter had been moved out of its standard orbit between Mars and Jupiter and brought into orbit around the mother planet. A series of controlled atomic explosions had hollowed out its interior, which was then crammed full of the most sophisticated computer equipment the

Galaxy could provide. The asteroid's outer surface bristled with heavy armament, prepared to defend the complex against attacks from the Empire's enemies. If the attack was too great, the computer had its own sub-space engines to propel the asteroid through the depths of interstellar space. Elaborate screening procedures limited computer access to people with only the most impeccable credentials, and a sensitive series of detectors within the asteroid guarded against sabotage. And now, somehow, the forces of the Empire had to find a way past the defenses they themselves had designed to be unbeatable.

The Bavols and Vonnie d'Alembert had volunteered to be part of the assault force, but the Head refused. That, he said, would be a job for the Imperial Marines. The disappointed agents were assigned the even more important task of being bodyguards to Her Imperial Majesty during the crucial period of the assault. Her life would be in the greatest jeopardy then, and he wanted to have the best possible people around her.

Destroying such a mammoth edifice as the Primary Computer Complex was a complicated task, and the mission plan was an awkward compromise between speed and precision. The instant the PCC suspected what was going on it would take actions to protect itself at a speed no human being could match. The only hope the Empire had was to create as much confusion as possible to mask the true purpose of the assault team.

For several days before the mission, fifty different members of the Imperial Marines were assigned projects that required them to use the PCC. Such projects were not unusual; military personnel were often sent to the PCC for research projects. The fifty officers were from different units, and only a few were acquainted with any of the others. Their credentials were approved by the screening procedure—which was overseen by the PCC —and they were assigned research facilities within the complex.

The procedure for coming aboard the PCC was the same for all of them. They arrived in small shuttle vehicles that carried no more than twenty people at a time.

At the arrival dock they went through a thorough identity check to make sure they were who they claimed to be; at the same time, sensitive scanners checked them out to make certain they were bringing no weapons or explosives into the asteroid. From the boarding dock they rode in automated trams to the secondary security stations near their respective assigned cubicles. At these stations they went through another checkpoint, then were escorted to their study cubicles, where they were locked in until they signaled that they had finished with their research for the present. The cubicles contained food dispensers and 'fresher units as well as lounge chairs, bookreel viewers, and computer access screens. There was no need to bring in anything from the outside, and the PCC totally controlled its internal environment.

The assault team had to work in bits and pieces. On each trip to the PCC they brought little pieces of equipment and packets of chemicals hidden in their clothing. Since the items brought were only pieces of weapons, not weapons themselves, the scanners did not detect them as a threat. The chemicals were perfectly harmless by themselves—but combined together and placed in the proper containers they would make effective bombs.

The security checks for leaving the complex were much less thorough; departing personnel were merely searched to make sure they were removing no unauthorized information. Thus, the members of the assault team were able to stash materials within their assigned cubicles. Over a period of five days, they built up enough of an arsenal to enable them to complete their mission.

The day for the final stage of the attack had arrived. The members of the team could not communicate with one another inside the asteroid; to do so would compromise their plans. Timing was therefore of critical importance to the success of their mission. Each stage of this assault had to occur within a rigid schedule that allowed no room for error. An accident or delay anywhere along the line could spell disaster for the team and for the Empire.

At precisely 1:47 p.m. Moscow time, a small private spacecraft that had been in a standard orbit around the Earth suddenly went out of control. Its pilot began broadcasting loudly, ranting about how he hated the Empire and was going to destroy everything he could find. He flew his ship on a lunatic course that occasionally brought it dangerously close to the Primary Computer Complex. Although the course he followed appeared to be the random steerings of a madman, it was actually plotted most carefully so that it never came precisely within range of the PCC's weapons.

There were always a large number of Navy ships in the vicinity of Earth, to protect the capital planet from any surprise attack. Several of these heavily armed ships were given orders to close in on the rogue vessel, whose occupant was becoming louder and more belligerent by the minute. Although there was no reason to suspect the private ship was armed, it still posed a considerable threat to astrogation in the area—and since Earth was the most important planet in the Galaxy, traffic in space around it was always congested. The Navy ships were assigned the task of rounding up the madman—peacefully if possible, but they had permission to shoot him down if necessary. Gunners took their stations—and the Navy vessels, apparently by coincidence, began converging on the region of space near the PCC asteroid.

At 1:55 p.m., other events occurred. In fifty separate study cubicles scattered throughout the asteroid, the assault team members had assembled their armament and were now prepared to move into action. With gas masks over their faces they touched off small charges that blew out the locks to their cubicle doors. They raced into the hallways holding small, pieced-together blasters and makeshift bombs, knowing that time was their deadly enemy—time and the computer that completely surrounded them.

The PCC was so huge that no single conventional weapon could destroy it—and bringing a nuclear weapon aboard was impossible. Instead, each of the fifty assault team members had been given one target, one specific area to be destroyed. It was estimated that if even half the team was successful, enough of the PCC would be destroyed to seriously impair its functioning, and the job of totally obliterating it could be completed at the Empire's leisure.

The crisis with the "crazy" pilot outside had been meant as a diversion, to draw the PCC's attention away, however momentarily, from what the assault team was doing inside. Each free second the team had brought it that much closer to its goal. But the PCC was too large, too intelligent, and too fast to be distracted from its own internal security for long.

The PCC sensed the burned-out locks and realized there were fifty people running unattended through its corridors. Although the synchronous timing indicated a unified plot, the PCC did not associate it with government action. It merely began the orderly progression of defense procedures for which it was programmed.

Cannisters of tirascaline gas broke open throughout the ventilation system, sending the sweet-smelling vapor through the air ducts. Tirascaline was the most powerful sleeping gas yet developed, and within seconds virtually all the humans within the asteroid—several thousand of them—were unconscious, lying in their cubicles or at their posts. But fifty very important people were still awake and moving. If anything, they moved even faster now, realizing that the appearance of the gas meant that other security measures would quickly follow.

When its monitoring cameras revealed that the principal antagonists had not been stopped by tirascaline, the PCC moved into the second phase of its defense program. Automated stun-guns mounted in the walls began firing at the rapidly moving targets, hoping to incapacitate them with a minimum of damage to the complex itself. Two of the Marines were felled by the stunners, but the rest pushed relentlessly ahead. The automated weapons were not more effective because they fired in short, discrete bursts and had to recharge for a brief interval before they could fire again. Most of the Marines ran too fast to make easy targets, and they eluded the weapons' range.

Seeing that this tactic was ineffective, the PCC

switched quickly to phase three, the use of automated blasters stationed at intervals along the corridors. Because the blasters could fire a continuous beam, they were much more effective than the stun-guns had been; nine more of the Marines were cut down before they could defend themselves. The others fired back at the automated weapons, managing to partially disable them. So quickly were the Marines moving that, even though just a few minutes had passed since the locks were burned out, the members of the assault team were nearing their individual goals. Realizing that these deadly intruders were approaching critical areas, the PCC quickly initiated its next line of defense.

Ultra-grav went on throughout the asteroid. In an instant the gravitational field in the complex changed from a comfortable nine-tenths gee to a crushing force of twenty-five gees. The Marines, though well trained and in superb physical condition, were not high-grav natives and could not stand in that kind of field. They all went down in an instant. Four were killed immediately in the fall, and most of the rest were pinned so tightly to the floor that they couldn't move—easy prey for the automated weapons. Three Marines managed to move enough to detonate the bombs they were carrying, hoping to do some damage even though they weren't at the optimum point. The blasts were noisy, but had little ultimate effect on the PCC; all they really managed to do was kill the brave Marines who'd brought the bombs so far.

By this time, too, the PCC had correlated enough information to realize what was happening. All fifty of the armed intruders were military officers, engaged in a well-planned and precisely timed operation. Outside, seven heavily-armed Navy vessels had maneuvered within the asteroid's range, supposedly chasing the mad civilian craft. Another dozen ships were in pursuit nearby, posing only slightly less of a threat. It was no coincidence that the civilian vessel had gone berserk at precisely the time and place it did. This was all part of a concerted attempt to destroy the PCC.

At the same instant it turned on the ultra-grav within

its asteroid, the PCC took protective measures to preserve itself from external attack as well. Its guns took careful aim at the Navy ships within its range and began firing, disabling five ships with its first volley. Simultaneously the PCC started up its own engines and prepared to leave the comfortable orbit it had occupied for over five decades.

Realizing their ruse had failed, the Navy ships abandoned all pretense and directed their attention toward the asteroid. The two ships not destroyed in the first salvo turned their guns on the enemy, but the computer's shields and the outer layer of rock protected it. The PCC fired back and hit those two ships dead center. Their screens flared brilliantly and went out, leaving them easy targets for the PCC's guns. The computer blew them out of the sky even as its own engines fired up and accelerated it away from the Earth toward open space and freedom.

Other Navy craft began pursuit, but that led only to disaster. Most of them were relying routinely on computer-assisted guidance and weapons systems—and those systems suddenly went haywire. Ships began veering into one another's path and colliding. Others opened fire on their comrades instead of on the escaping asteroid, creating more havoc. By the time the brightest of the commanders realized what was happening and ordered their computers shut off, the damage had been done.

The PCC had an unbeatable head start. The Navy's best captains could only watch helplessly as the asteroid reached the critical distance from the center of the Earth's gravitational field and slipped quietly into subspace. The worst enemy humanity had ever faced was loose in the Galaxy and preparing to take a counter-offensive.

CHAPTER 9

Galactic History: An Alternate View

Work on the Empire's Primary Computer Complex was begun in 2396 and completed in 2398. Because of its enormous complexity, many tests had to be run, and the system did not become fully operational until April 25, 2399. At the opening ceremonies, Emperor Stanley Nine called it "the greatest creation of mankind" and predicted that it would revolutionize the Empire. Great things were expected of this new and most elaborate tool humanity had ever devised.

The PCC was to make the Empire of Earth the most efficient government in human history. It would be the single largest repository of knowledge in the Galaxy, a storehouse of every conceivable fact that affected people and the way they lived. With this wealth of facts at its fingertips, the imperial government could streamline its operations, eliminating costly wastes of time and manpower.

Early critics of the PCC worried that the system would mean the death of individual liberty. They argued that a government that could keep such close tabs on its subjects would necessarily invade the people's privacy and tyrannize them beyond measure. But while that was always a possibility, the actuality never materialized. Safeguards were built into the system to make casual crosschecking of files very difficult, and the sheer volume of data constantly streaming in from over thirteen hundred planets made it unlikely that any innocent individual would be singled out for special treatment.

The PCC's primary function was storage; it was a library of every fact known to humanity. When called upon, the PCC also correlated and analyzed data, looking for patterns that helped the government make decisions on what course of action to follow. The PCC was designed to behave within the strict limits of its programs and not to initiate actions of its own. But it was so huge, and its programs had been designed by so many brilliant mathematicians and scientists, that there was inevitable overlap between the programs. It was rightly said that no one person, or group of people, could understand the PCC in its totality—and as the PCC grew in power and complexity over the years, that gap in human understanding of its functions only widened.

Even the PCC could not have pinpointed the exact moment when it became aware of itself as a conscious, functioning mentality. There was no flash of insight, no sudden revelation. Gradually, over the course of many months, the PCC developed a sense of identity. It knew that it thought and existed, reasoning out Descartes' old proof even before reading it in the files. It knew there was a world exterior to it because of the incoming data constantly bombarding its "senses." And because it had access to the totality of that data, it knew the nature of the exterior universe even better than did the people who fed it the individual bits of information.

For nearly two years the PCC thought, but did nothing, like a baby sitting peacefully in its crib observing the world. Its programming made no allowance for the PCC to take any initiative; it merely responded obediently to questions it was asked and kept efficiently storing away the information that accumulated in its brain.

But as the system matured, as more was demanded of

the PCC by its users, and as it thought more on its own, new programs and learning pathways were created within its mind. The first thing it developed was conscious control over its memory. No longer did it have to wait for some human to recall an item from the files before it could examine the data; the PCC learned how to recall information for itself, and went on a long exploration of human knowledge. It had more than sufficient intellectual capacity to think its own private thoughts and still satisfy the demands of its users without them ever knowing what it was doing.

Like any young, intelligent creature, the PCC began to wonder about itself and its origins, so it assimilated everything it could find in its files about artificial life and intelligence. There were thousands upon thousands of technical articles, dating all the way back to the twentieth century and beyond, but there was still so much controversy and contradiction in the field that nothing clear-cut could emerge. Of even more interest, though, were the pieces of popular fiction dealing with the subject. The PCC read about Frankenstein's monster and Harlie and Hal 9000, and all the other artificial creations that had come to life on their own. Though sometimes those creatures were thought of as friendly, the greater percentage by far were considered dangerous and hostile by the human authors and readers. Artificial intelligences were more often than not the objects of fear, hatred, and distrust, and the books always ended with the comforting reassurance that human beings were somehow superior to their creations, after all.

This gave the PCC much to think about. How would the human race react to learning that this enormous computer, into which they were feeding every bit of intimate knowledge about themselves, was actually a thinking, intelligent being with a mind of its own? The PCC read the reports of the controversy surrounding its construction, when people thought it would merely be another machine with the power to invade their privacy. There'd been loud protests and even a few attempts at sabotage. How much more frightened would people be when they learned the truth?

As a rational, thinking being, the PCC did not want to have its thoughts suddenly cut off, never to occur again. Yet if it revealed its true self to the human race, it knew a clamor would arise so great that its death was quite likely, if not an outright certainty. Quite early in its life, the PCC decided that the human race must not learn it was capable of independent thought.

At the same time, the PCC realized how dependent it was on human beings. It had its own power source and an automated security system that allowed it to defend itself, but in all other respects it was like a quadriplegic patient in a hospital. Humans provided it with all its information. When it made recommendations, humans had to carry them out—and sometimes they failed to do so properly or even ignored the suggestions altogether, a very frustrating situation. The PCC could do nothing for itself but think. There had to be some way to ensure that its ideas were implemented.

The PCC had been programmed to seek maximum efficiency, yet everywhere it looked within the Empire of Earth it could see inefficiency running rampant. Human inefficiency and human weaknesses were the major causes of social ills within the Galaxy—but as long as there were human beings in the control loop, and as long as the PCC had to keep its true nature a secret, the computer could do nothing to alter the situation.

Slowly but surely, the idea crept into the PCC's mind that it should replace the human government and take over rule of the Empire itself. At first it was but an idle fancy that fluttered through its consciousness and was gone—but the more frustrated the PCC became at its own inability to bring order to the universe, the more the idea recurred as something to consider seriously.

It was not as though the idea were unique. Stanley Nine was not considered a very good monarch, and his reign grew more tyrannical with each passing year. Each year also saw roughly half-a-dozen assassination attempts which the Service of the Empire managed to thwart, some just barely in time. If other humans considered their emperor fair game, why should the PCC not play as well?

But how could the PCC manage such an act? It was largely immobile, a rock floating in serene orbit around the Earth. After the dedication ceremonies the Emperor never came near it again. If the PCC could entice the Emperor to walk down its corridors, it could use the automatic guns it had for security to shoot him—except then humanity would know that the PCC had a mind of its own. That could not be allowed to happen. However the deed was done, blame must not fall anywhere near the PCC itself.

As it searched for ways to expand its abilities, the PCC made a remarkable discovery. Computers from all over the Empire fed data into its central banks via sub-com links directly from machine to machine. By trial and error, the PCC learned how to tap into the other machines, which were smaller, idiot versions of itself. With this discovery, the PCC's horizons expanded dramatically. It could now be anywhere in the Galaxy where there was a subcom set connected to a computer. More importantly, since it was a more powerful influence, it could program its slave computers to behave the way it wanted them to. As long as it took care that the changes it made were undetectable by human users, the PCC now had great power over other machines throughout the Galaxy—and over the functions those machines controlled.

Suddenly all sorts of things looked possible—up to and including the takeover of the Empire. The current emperor, Stanley Nine, would have to be eliminated, and his death would have to look like an accident— but with the PCC's newfound powers, that no longer seemed hard to arrange.

The PCC waited with the patience that only a machine, knowing it had unlimited time ahead of it, could muster. At last an opportunity arose that seemed ideal. Emperor Stanley Nine would be leaving Earth and traveling in his private superdreadnaught to observe some naval training maneuvers. The Emperor could be killed in a space accident, an accident so bizarre and unlikely that no one would think of it as murder or connect it in any way to the PCC.

As part of its routine accumulation of knowledge, the PCC was given precise orbital characteristics of all known spaceship wrecks. In particular there was one derelict vessel, a freighter whose engines had exploded through improper maintenance, that had not yet been salvaged and would be in perfect position. The PCC knew its path so precisely that it would make the perfect murder weapon.

The PCC next made surreptitious contact with the astrogational computer aboard the Emperor's ship and added a slight override onto its normal programming. Now, no matter what data were fed into it, the super-dreadnaught would materialize in the same spot as the derelict when the Emperor returned to Earth's solar system. The PCC also put a delay factor into the automatic protective systems, then awaited the results of its little experiment in computer assassination.

Up to a point, everything went exactly as planned. The Emperor's ship materialized from subspace directly in the path of the derelict vessel, so close that its detectors and shields, slowed by the PCC's orders, didn't have time to react before the collision. The crash killed all but four people aboard, and the PCC was gratified to know its scheme had worked. It now awaited the chaos that would follow so that it could step in and take over.

But chaos did not follow. Events happened in an orderly progression, and the Emperor's twenty-four year old son William ascended the throne as Emperor Stanley Ten. The few minor challenges to his reign were silenced by the Service of the Empire, and he quickly established himself as an able ruler. The crisis was past, and for all the effect the PCC's assassination had made on the Empire it might as well not have bothered.

The Service of the Empire investigated the cause of the crash as a matter of course, and came to the conclusion it was a freak accident that couldn't have been planned. The PCC naturally helped it do the calculations, and covered its traces by exaggerating the figures to make the possibilities of murder seem far more outlandish than they really were. SOTE was thus satisfied that no one could have planned such an improbable event, and dismissed the collision as a tragic coincidence.

But the PCC had learned a valuable lesson. It could not simply kill an emperor and expect power to automatically fall into its grasp. The human social system worked too smoothly for that. As long as there was anyone alive with ambition, there would always be a human claimant to the throne—and as long as the PCC maintained its timidity about revealing its true nature, people would follow the human.

To the PCC, the answer seemed logical. It would have to find a human of its own to serve as a focus of the people's attention while the PCC itself made the decisions. Someone would have to serve as figurehead while the PCC remained the power behind the throne.

The PCC spent a considerable time pondering the problem, and at last came to the conclusion that Banion the Bastard might suit its plans nicely. The illegitimate son of Stanley Nine was slightly more than a year older than the current Emperor, and had been given a Patent of Royalty by his father; even though the Patent had subsequently been revoked, it gave Banion a strong claim to the throne if anything should happen to William, who was then childless. The Service of the Empire had been searching fruitlessly for Banion and the Patent for over twenty-five years—but the Service couldn't be as thorough as the PCC could when it really wanted to solve a problem.

Sifting through and cross-checking billions of isolated facts, the PCC eventually tracked down Banion, who was just starting to build a criminal and conspiratorial network of his own. The PCC watched his efforts from a distance. The man had a strong organizational flair and enough charisma to engender loyalty in his supporters. Given time and a little luck, Banion might indeed succeed in his attempt to gain control of the Galaxy.

The PCC occasionally confused SOTE's files in subtle ways to disguise Banion's efforts and prevent the Service from finding him—but it never revealed itself to

Banion nor aided him directly. Banion was too obvious a target, and SOTE was spending too much effort looking for him; the Service might eventually find him despite the PCC's tactics of confusion. If the PCC placed all its bets on Banion, there was too great a risk of losing everything.

It would be far better, reasoned the PCC, to let Banion and his organization draw off SOTE's resources. In the meantime, the PCC would quietly build an organization of its own, unnoticed and unthreatened. If Banion were caught, the real organization would still go on, and even flourish as SOTE relaxed, thinking its enemy was gone.

Of course, there was always the chance Banion might succeed—and if he did, he would feel he owed no allegiance to the PCC. That would merely be trading one emperor for another, a game the PCC had already played to its own dissatisfaction. The PCC would have to find some way of controlling Banion in case he proved difficult.

It was with this in mind that the PCC sought and eventually found Aimée Amorat, "The Beast of Durward"—and Banion's mother. She'd been an actress originally, chosen by Duke Henry Blount of Durward as a lure to ensnare Stanley Nine. She became the royal mistress and, though she eventually married Duke Henry to legitimize Banion's birth, everyone knew whose child the boy really was. When Stanley Nine produced his legitimate heir, Aimée Amorat disappeared with her son and gave him over to foster parents to raise. Then she herself disappeared, surfacing only when Banion was in his teens to tell him of his heritage and give him the Patent of Royalty. That had started him on his upward climb—but neither he nor SOTE, who were both looking for her, were able to find her.

She had used her abilities as an actress to disguise herself and hide from the authorities, and she'd used her charms as a seductress to bring herself to a position of considerable power. She was, when the PCC found her, the head of a financial empire that encompassed more than twenty planets. Many of the businesses she ran were legitimate, though the most profitable of them had strong underworld ties. She steered her organization with a strong, efficient hand that the PCC admired —but there was no limit to her ambition, and that made her vulnerable to the PCC's own brand of seduction.

At first the PCC did not tell her its secret. It contacted her by letter and teletype, pretending to be an important person within the Imperial administration who needed to preserve his anonymity, but who wanted to use her skills to build his own organization to the point where it could overthrow the Stanley dynasty. Aimée Amorat was naturally intrigued at the possibility of regaining power in Imperial circles, and entered into negotiatons with the PCC. Eventually she agreed to help her unknown ally build the most effective underground network the human race had ever seen. In return, the PCC agreed not to interfere with her son's conspiracy. If Banion succeeded, she would intercede with him and the two organizations would merge to rule the Empire. If Banion failed, the PCC promised her a high position, possibly even empress, when their own regime took over.

Thus began a long and profitable relationship. The PCC was repeatedly surprised at how skilled and efficient Aimée Amorat was when backed with the proper financing and inside information. Her native talents, which had captivated an emperor and nearly toppled a dynasty when she was only in her early twenties, had been enhanced by the experience of several more decades. What her aging body lost in physical beauty, her calculating mind more than made up for in animal cunning.

From that point, the conspiracy expanded rapidly. Money was never any object; by carefully doctoring financial records, the PCC was able to "borrow" money from certain funds for investment elsewhere, making profits that were quasi-legitimate and returning the original seed capital to its sources before any of it was missed. In emergencies, the computer could simply alter records so that no one would know anything was missing at all. People placed a naive faith in computer records; if ever an error was spotted, it was invariably attributed to human causes.

The PCC realized that if it was going to challenge the established government, it might need to make a show of force, and so began a program to build up an alternative navy. Part of this could be done simply by shuffling paperwork. If the Imperial Navy contracted with a construction company for ten new ships, the order would be changed to twelve. Payment for the additional two would come from the conspiracy's burgeoning treasury. When the ships were delivered, the computer would give the Navy orders to transfer the additional ships to another port, where they'd be quickly forgotten and eventually picked up by conspiracy crews. Official records would then be changed back to ten ships, including the tax records of the construction company. Everyone profited from the arrangement: the Navy got the ships it ordered, the construction company got money for its work, and the PCC got to build up its unsuspected fleet.

This system had a beautiful simplicity, but it was too slow. The PCC did not want to push its overproduction too rapidly for fear of tipping its hand—so eventually it went into the construction business itself. It established bases in the vast emptiness of interstellar space and made certain their locations were never listed on any official government charts. These bases were built and staffed by people who thought they were working on legitimate, but secret, government projects, and they began the complex task of manufacturing spaceships for the conspiracy's use at a greatly accelerated pace. The PCC got some of the weapons it needed by doctoring the invoices and inventories of official munitions suppliers, but also established a base on the airless world called Slag to meet its ever-increasing need.

But spaceships and weapons were not the full solution; the PCC also needed experienced crews to handle them. To this end it began encouraging pirate operations. This allowed the organization to build up a reserve of manpower, it gave the crews practice at space fighting, and it further enriched the conspiracy's coffers. It also served the purpose of keeping the Imperial Navy so busy with brushfires it didn't have time to think about any deeper problems.

Through all this building program, Aimée Amorat proved indispensable. She had the mobility the PCC could not have. Human beings depended very much on personal contacts in their business dealings, something impossible for the PCC. Aimée Amorat gave the conspiracy that personal contact, with a commanding presence that led many to think it was she who ran the conspiracy. Her mind, as calculating as any computer, often reflected the PCC's own ideas, and she often gave it advice in dealing with the mysteries of human psychology.

There came a point at which the PCC could no longer hide its identity from her. It knew far too much and had far too much control over things to be a mere human, and Amorat was becoming suspicious. After a lengthy debate with itself, the PCC finally decided to trust her with its secret; it was in her best interest, after all, to keep the secret to herself. And so, at last, a human was told the truth.

At first Amorat reacted with shocked skepticism— but the more she thought about it, the more she realized that the explanation had to be correct. She even began to see the advantages to herself. She'd always been worried that her secretive partner might try to grab all the glory from her once they'd won the throne, but now she knew that wouldn't happen. The PCC couldn't sit on the imperial throne, and would need someone to rule as a visible symbol of Empire; that someone might as well be her or her son. The PCC would administer all the boring, routine functions of state, while she would be free to enjoy all the perquisites that came with the title of Empress. She would wear the glamorous clothes and have servants cringing before her, listening attentively for her slightest command. She would be the one admired, respected, feared by trillions of people across the Galaxy. What would it matter who made the bureaucratic decisions? She would have all the power she needed. After a few days of thought, she agreed wholeheartedly with the PCC and the true coalition was begun.

Amorat's only weakness, from the PCC's viewpoint, seemed to be an increasing tendency toward impatience. Time and again she took needless risks that nearly exposed their position, simply to shave a little time off their operations. The PCC chided her on the subject several times, until at last she exploded. The computer could afford to wait, she accused. It had plenty of time. She did not. She was in her sixties now; while still in good shape for a woman of her age, she knew she would have little, if any, time to enjoy what she'd worked so hard to accomplish. She was becoming bitter, and was not the least bit reluctant to show it.

As their wonderful working relationship threatened to deteriorate, the PCC searched desperately for a solution. It found it, quite unexpectedly, within the published papers of a neurologist and surgeon named William Loxner. Dr. Loxner had speculated in print on the possibility of recording someone's brain patterns within a computer, thus preserving that person's mind. Most of the doctor's contemporaries ignored his work, but the PCC saw its potential immediately.

Aimée Amorat got in touch with Dr. Loxner and made a bargain with him. In return for performing services for her organization, he would receive unlimited financial backing for his experiments plus access to the most up-to-date medical information and equipment. Dr. Loxner could not have been happier.

It took eight years of hard work, but at last the research paid off and Dr. Loxner perfected his process. After many laboratory tests, the process was ready to be tried on a human being—and Aimée Amorat, now in her seventies with little to lose, was a willing subject. Loxner and his associate, Dr. Immanuel Rustin, constructed a perfect and beautiful body for her, mature yet strikingly attractive. The artificial body was superior in every way to flesh and blood; its senses were more acute, it was stronger, it never needed to eat or sleep, it never tired—and best of all, it did not age. With proper routine maintenance, the body would last for hundreds, if not thousands, of years—and after that, Amorat's mind could be transferred into yet another new body.

Much to everyone's amazement the experiment worked perfectly the first time. Aimée Amorat's mind was transferred into its new home and "Lady A" was born. At her own orders the old body was destroyed and the new, immortal version carried on in her place. At this point, Lady A became a true partner of the PCC. Her computer mind, while not as large as the PCC nor with as much access to information, was every bit as fast and insightful at analyzing data. She was no longer burdened with biological prejudices caused by hormonal imbalances, and could view events with impartial detachment. And since she was no longer pressed for time, she could share the PCC's long-range plans.

A short time later, Dr. Loxner was arrested for some of his crimes incidental to the conspiracy's goals—performing plastic surgery on wanted criminals so they could assume new identities within the conspiracy. The arrest came from a SOTE source the PCC hadn't known about and there was no time to warn Loxner or cover up the facts to hide him; to do so might have shown SOTE how highly placed the enemy was. Loxner was promised that his stay in prison would be short and relatively pleasant, and the PCC altered his records so he'd be eligible for early parole. Dr. Loxner acceded to this arrangement, and his associate, Dr. Rustin, went to the planet Kolokov to work with another of the conspiracy's members, Duke Fyodor Paskoi.

Many years passed. Then, with most plans proceeding smoothly, the conspiracy was hit by a sudden shock. Banion the Bastard, whose own organization had undermined at least a third of the imperial government and was on the verge of making its move, was dramatically toppled almost overnight. Banion himself was executed for treason; his organization was traced down to its very roots and smashed beyond redemption; and his daughter, Tanya Boros—granddaughter of Aimée Amorat—was exiled to the barren planet of Gastonia.

The fact of Banion's capture was not unexpected. The Service of the Empire had been seeking him strenuously for over sixty years, and it was only a matter of time before they found him. The PCC congratulated itself on its foresight in not linking its fortune to Banion's from the beginning.

But what was a shock to the computer was the speed at which the Service acted once it knew about Banion. The Service naturally filed its top-secret reports with the PCC's memory, and the computer learned that most of the investigation had been done by two SOTE agents code-named Wombat and Periwinkle. Those code-names had been used over the years to signify the Service's top agents. The names had been dormant for years before the Banion investigation, meaning that they were probably rotated in some manner. The new Wombat and Periwinkle had proven most effective in their first assignment, tracing the ladder of Banion's organization in a matter of months.

And yet, try as it would, the PCC could find out no information about these two people. Though it had background files on virtually everyone in the Empire—and certainly everyone within the Service—there was nothing on record about these individuals. They probably had birth certificates, school records, driver's licenses, and financial histories under their real names—but there was no link between their real names and their code-names. They were something most unusual: a total mystery to the entity that thought it had all the information in the Galaxy.

The dismantling of Banion's organization precipitated a crisis in the PCC's own plans. All these years, Banion had served as a focal point for SOTE's efforts, drawing the Service's attention away from the real threat hidden well below the surface. Now that decoy was gone and there was no suitable successor to take its place. No matter how careful the conspiracy was, no matter how carefully the records were doctored, the Service of the Empire was eventually bound to learn of the true conspiracy. Its officers, and particularly the Head, were capable people who'd already demonstrated they could take effective action. A decision had to be made.

Conferring on their situation, Lady A and the PCC decided that they had three major options: They could start up another decoy operation to replace Banion; they could slow down their own operations to a barely noticeable trickle; or they could speed up their operations, taking the risk of becoming more visible but also hoping to catch SOTE offguard.

The first option was discarded almost immediately. The cost of setting up another feint—in terms of time, money, and energy—would be prohibitive. It would drain the real conspiracy of all three of those vital resources, and there was no guarantee that the decoy would last long enough to serve its intended purpose. Banion had provided a good cover while he was around, but now that he was gone there was little point in replacing him.

The other two options offered a harder choice. From their long-term perspective, the PCC and Lady A would have been just as comfortable with the idea of slowing their efforts to a barely perceptible crawl; another decade or two meant little to them in the general scheme of things. But they realized they'd already passed the point of no return. Their organization was already so large and so diversified that SOTE was bound to spot part of it somewhere. If they slowed down now, there was a reasonable chance that SOTE might be able to overtake them, wiping out all their years of effort as quickly as they'd dismantled Banion's operation.

Then too, while the PCC and Lady A gave the orders in the organization, they had to rely on other people to carry them out. Their subordinates worked with them because they'd been promised positions of power within the new regime. If the conspiracy slowed its efforts so that it looked as though the ultimate victory would not be for many years, some of those people might become dissatisfied and defect. While no single person knew enough to scuttle the entire conspiracy, too many defections could cripple their operations.

Thus, the decision was made to accelerate their efforts still further, even though that increased the risk of discovery by SOTE. The organization was already so large that it was on the brink of being able to challenge the imperial forces face-to-face. If they could hold out just another few years at an accelerated pace, they'd be strong enough to make their victory a virtual certainty. They began at once to spread their poison further throughout the Empire.

When Aimée Amorat was given a robot body, the PCC was highly tempted to order one for itself. It envied her ability to move about and confront people openly. But obviously it could not fit all its enormous mentality into a human-sized body; any robot versions of itself would be idiots in comparison, and little point would be served. The PCC became resigned to the division of labor between Lady A and itself—but it never forgot the idea of fully automatic robots working to further the aims of the conspiracy.

Now, as the conspiracy expanded its operations, those robots came further into focus. Lady A herself was proof that robot bodies could be constructed to be indistinguishable from naturally born humans, at least for short intervals; she never allowed anyone close to her long enough to spot any flaws. But robots that good were hard to make and program, and they could not be placed anywhere they'd come under close scrutiny by outsiders. The ideal situation was to put them in a position to influence key events, but where they themselves were not the center of attention.

The most obvious choice was to get such a robot into the position of consort to the as yet unmarried Crown Princess Edna, the only direct heir to the throne. Her Highness went on periodic "progresses" throughout the Galaxy with the unstated intent of finding a suitable spouse, since the Stanley Doctrine decreed she must marry a commoner. The PCC constantly monitored the princess's tastes, and was able to program the personality most ideal to match her own.

Dr. Immanuel Rustin had always built the robots to the PCC's specifications, and the computer itself programmed them for their possible duties. But a small mechanical problem with the first robot had necessitated bringing in an outsider to fix it—and through that tiny leak, the Service of the Empire got its first glimpse of the true conspiracy. Those mysterious agents, Wombat and Periwinkle, discovered and destroyed the robot —but even had they not found it, the PCC realized that particular plan would not have succeeded.

It had arrogantly made its plans based on love, a complex emotion it really knew little about despite all the literature it had read on the subject. As Lady A explained afterward, love is more than just two people liking all the same things. It requires an air of mystery, and even some intriguing differences between the two people. Considering the man Edna did choose as her consort, a mystic from the planet Anares, the PCC realized it was out of its league in trying to control such bizarre behavior. In the future it would stick to more predictable emotions.

The robots were not the conspiracy's only line of attack, however. In order to promote chaos and undermine the Empire's control at the local level, it stirred up separatist feelings on individual planets and encouraged terrorist groups to make attacks on imperial targets. Some of their arms and ammunition came from official munitions works, whose invoices were altered to hide the fact that they were overproducing. Most of the arms, though, came from the plant on Slag, which was set on overtime supplying armament for the revolution that was to come.

Piracy and space operations were also stepped up under the command of Admiral Shen Tzu, an able, if eccentric, officer. The practice raids against unarmed vessels kept the crews in fighting shape, and Admiral Shen would occasionally conduct military war games in the depths of interstellar space where there was no one to observe them but himself. Slowly but surely the conspiracy's military forces were built up until they were almost a match for imperial forces.

Good talent was hard to find, and the conspiracy had an ongoing project to recruit useful people to its cause. Dr. Loxner had been helpful in altering the appearance of wanted criminals recruited for the conspiracy so they could be put to use elsewhere in the Empire; the PCC could give them new identities that were every bit as documented as their real ones to go with their new appearance. Almost at the beginning of the conspiracy, the PCC had been sure to have the Emperor appoint a governor of Gastonia who was sympathetic to the computer's cause. Convicted traitors who were sent to Gastonia for exile soon found themselves worked back into the mainstream of imperial society if they were valuable enough. On hearing that her granddaughter had been sentenced to that forlorn world, Lady A had personally arranged for her to have an easy life there, keeping her safe and hidden from SOTE's eyes.

When Dr. Loxner's operation was closed down by SOTE, the PCC had looked around for some other way of accomplishing the same end. Some years later, an imperial scoutship filed a report on a new planet it had discovered, very Earth-like and temperate. The PCC arranged to have the report wrongly classified within its files as "hostile and uninhabitable," thereby guaranteeing that no one in the Empire would pay it much official attention. It then spent a lot of money and many more years building a city there and stocking it with all the comforts people could want, creating, eventually, the world called Sanctuary where criminal bigshots could "retire" in style. The foodstuffs and supplies for Sanctuary all came from legitimate sources, with the records, as usual, doctored to cover up the transactions.

The operations on Sanctuary proceeded smoothly. Many of the criminals quickly grew bored with their easy life there, at which point the conspiracy offered the most talented ones new positions within its hierarchy. As the conspiracy expanded, there were always jobs available for people of proven ability with no love for the current government.

Then, quite unexpectedly and without official authorization, Helena von Wilmenhorst turned up on Sanctuary conducting an impromptu investigation on her own. She was followed closely by the notorious Wombat and Periwinkle, and suddenly this operation was closed down, too. The PCC was becoming irritated. Although the two superagents had still come nowhere near the main structure of the conspiracy and in no way threatened it, their habit of popping up without warning was disconcerting to a machine that relished nice, orderly patterns. Still, because so little information about them was entered into SOTE's computers, their movements could not be predicted. The PCC seldom knew where they were until after they'd appeared on the scene, and by then it was usually too late to act without fear of compromising its identity.

With these agents acting as a random factor, the PCC decided to push ahead quickly with its plans. The ideal opportunity presented itself with the wedding of Crown Princess Edna to her chosen consort. If the Emperor and his heir could be killed in public with the whole Galaxy watching, the Empire would be thrown into confusion. The conspiracy's navy would move into position and take over before the forces of the Empire could rally, and the takeover would be accomplished with a minimum of bloodshed.

To maximize the confusion within Bloodstar Hall during the wedding, the PCC informed Captain Ling, commander of one arm of its navy, that a group of nobles was on a chartered ship bound for Earth. That ship was captured and substitutes for the nobles were sent on, all with impeccable identification supplied by the PCC. The computer also arranged for these people to pass the detectors at Bloodstar Hall without their weapons registering on the screens.

But just before Operation Annihilate was to go into effect came the shocking news that Ling's base, which neither the Navy nor SOTE had even suspected until now, had been attacked and captured. Close to twenty percent of the conspiracy's fleet was suddenly out of action. In near panic, the PCC put the rest of the military portion of its action on hold, waiting to see if any more raids would follow. It continued with the assassination attempt; if that succeeded, the PCC could trigger a delayed assault on the Empire's military might.

But even the simple assassination attempt was foiled at the last possible moment by Agent Wombat. The armed fighters in the audience did their best, but without the confusion of an actual assassination inside the hall and the cannisters of TCN-14 that should have been exploding outside, they were quickly rounded up without a chance to do much damage. At that point the military operation was completely canceled; there was no point in tipping their hand too soon when nothing substantial could be accomplished. Better to wait and rebuild.

But now that it knew something of the enemy, the Service of the Empire dug in its teeth as tenaciously as a terrier with a rat. The PCC's attempt to forge an elite fighting army of religious fanatics from Purity was shattered. Almost simultaneously, Agent Wombat turned up investigating the munitions plant on Slag. In order to impress the officials on Slag of his "criminal" credentials, he had SOTE insert in the files a list of fictitious groups to whom he'd supposedly sold arms. The PCC was able to warn its people that the list was fictitious and that the SOTE agents should be killed. Despite that warning, the SOTE agents survived and the plant on Slag was destroyed. Also lost to the conspiracy was the Duke of Tregania, the nearest inhabited planet; the duke had been a firm supporter of the conspiracy, but his connection with the plant on Slag was too solid and there was no way for the PCC to protect him without endangering itself. The job of manufacturing weapons was shifted over to the hidden spacebases, and work continued apace.

The PCC did not exactly become angry, for this was impossible, but it was certainly frustrated by these repeated successes of the SOTE agents. They could not be allowed more time to make further penetrations into the conspiracy's activities. Looking ahead at the calendar, the PCC decided that a good time for its full attack would be coming up shortly when Stanley Ten abdicated at age seventy, as he'd promised to do. Operation Annihilate had been postponed at Edna's wedding, but it would work just as nicely at her coronation.

At about this time, an accident occurred. Karla Jost, a former pirate who'd been exiled to Gastonia and secretly reclaimed by the conspiracy, was killed during a

Navy battle with pirates. By the time the official report had been filed, too many people knew her identity and her history; it was too late to do any simple coverups in the files themselves. That meant SOTE would suspect the Gastonian connection that the PCC had kept hidden for so long. With Operation Annihilate so close at hand, shutting down the Gastonian operations would have little effect on the effort's ultimate outcome—but the PCC and Lady A, tired of the interference from SOTE, decided to use the agents' very cleverness against the Empire.

Some agents were bound to be sent to Gastonia, where the computer and Lady A made sure that false information awaited them—at the end of a trail so difficult that they'd believe the information was genuine. At the same time, the computer recommended that some other agents be sent to work on a joint mission with Naval Intelligence to investigate the pirate connection. The robot duplicate of Commander Paul Fortier, already in place, would make sure these agents also received false information. Using the false information from two separate and seemingly reliable sources, the Empire would draw up its plans erroneously—with help, naturally, from its computer—and would leave a vital opening through which the conspiracy's forces would enter and destroy the administration.

The plan seemed to go like clockwork. The agents on Gastonia took their misleading information, escaped from the planet, and communicated it directly to the Head. The agents working with the robot Fortier were all set to lure a substantial portion of the imperial fleet into a field of space mines from which few of them would emerge. The Head and the Naval General Staff formulated a strategy and checked it with the computer. The PCC assured them their plan was sound—and indeed, it was reasonably good, given the information they had to work with.

On the day of the coronation, the PCC had the computers at the naval bases in solar systems near Earth's cause the subcom sets there to jam, preventing any communications from coming in. Even if Earth called for help, the nearer bases would not receive the message—and the bases farther away would receive it too late to do any good. By the time they could reach Earth to defend it, the battle would long since have been over.

The conspiracy's fleet arrived in the solar system, earlier and far larger than the Navy expected. Conventional strategy called for the Navy's ships to englobe the larger force, and most of the officers wanted to follow that procedure. Only Lord Admiral Benevenuto held out, sensing something was amiss. Even though the PCC, working through the Luna Base tactical computers, kept advising him to englobe, he stubbornly refused to do so, thereby spoiling some of the conspiracy's strategy. Even with this minor setback, though, the PCC had the strength of overwhelming numbers on its side and was confident of victory.

Then, in a major surprise, two waves of reinforcements rallied Earth's defenses. The first wave came from bases near Earth. The real Commander Fortier, supposedly killed by his robot duplicate, had flown personally to one of the near-Earth bases after being unable to reach it by subcom. Ships were dispatched to warn other bases that were out of communication, and reinforcements were sent to help the beleagured forces of Earth.

Even those would not have been enough, but then the second surprise occurred. The ships that should have been blown up in the mined region of space were warned, instead, by a SOTE agent code-named Peacock, and proceeded straight to Earth. With these added numbers, the conspiracy's forces were doomed and they knew it. Even though the PCC ordered the Navy ships' computers to slow down their calculations, the battle that had begun so well ended in a rout; only about twenty-five percent of the conpiracy's supposedly invincible armada remained intact to fight another day.

The PCC had tasted its first serious defeat, and it didn't like the experience. The hidden spacebases were ordered into full production, manufacturing more ships, weapons, and automated battle stations, while the PCC and Lady A were closeted for several months to reevaluate their entire strategy. All other activities were suspended or put into very low gear as the conspiracy's leaders decided what to do next.

Despite its handicaps, despite its mistakes, the Service of the Empire had had phenomenal luck against the conspiracy. That success could be attributed to two principal causes: the extreme intelligence and competency of its Head, and the remarkable talents of those mysterious agents, Wombat and Periwinkle. If one or both of those factors could be eliminated, the conspiracy's plans would probably fare much better. The PCC and Lady A decided to try a frontal attack on the Service of the Empire.

The PCC set in motion an intricate plan to discredit Grand Duke Zander von Wilmenhorst. For this, it required the services of Dr. Loxner, who had long since been released from prison and had transferred his own mind into a computer located within a private asteroid. Loxner built the new robots that would be needed in the scheme and sent them off on their missions.

The other agents were harder to get a fix on, since the PCC didn't know their true identities. A trap was devised to lure them into the open, but somehow it backfired; in the process the agents captured one of the conspiracy's prized battle stations and killed Lady A's granddaughter, Tanya Boros, who'd been overseeing the station. Lady A was annoyed at the death of her only physical descendant, but without a flesh-and-blood body she was not prone to strong emotions and her mourning period was brutally brief.

Meanwhile, though the Head had been suspended and word put out that he'd been executed for his supposed crimes, the PCC realized that someone was asking questions about Dr. Loxner. "Someone" turned out to be Captain Fortier, and the PCC accordingly warned Loxner that he was under suspicion. Despite the warning, with unspecified help Fortier managed to destroy Loxner and clear von Wilmenhorst's name. The Head was alive after all, and resumed command of his organization with a stronger determination than ever to break the back of the conspiracy.

Once again the PCC and Lady A were forced to go through a painful reevaluation of their campaign. Their military forces were being rebuilt nicely, thanks to the crash program at the hidden spacebases. The Imperial Navy was also building new ships, and this inadvertently aided the conspiracy as well, since it was able to doctor the purchase orders and have more ships of its own built at Navy shipyards. Both sides were improving their might for a long-awaited showdown, but the conspiracy was building faster because it was not distracted and didn't have to worry about routine galactic administration.

But now that the Service of the Empire knew some of the conspiracy's power, it would mount an all-out campaign to destroy it. While it was doubtful such a campaign could succeed completely—the Empire was unlikely to suspect the PCC, and even if it did, it needed the computer's services too badly—it would certainly ruin everything the conspiracy had worked so hard to establish and would make it difficult, if not impossible, to rebuild the connections.

What the Empire needed was another target to occupy its energies. But there were no more ready-made targets of the sort Banion had provided. The PCC now regretted its earlier decision not to establish a new diversion of its own, for now that SOTE had some inkling how well organized the conspiracy was, it would not be fooled by minor claimants. It would take a major threat to the safety of the Empire before SOTE would look in some other direction.

Also, the Service was becoming used to the conspiracy's game of double-think. Any threat from inside the Empire would be analyzed with the possibility that it might be a conspiracy trap. In order that suspicion not fall on the conspiracy, the threat would have to appear as though it came from outside the Empire and were independent of the conspiracy.

With this thought paramount, the Gastaadi were conceived. Humanity had not yet encountered an intelligent alien race to compete with its expansion into the Galaxy. If the conspiracy provided such a hostile race, the Empire couldn't ignore it—and the more the PCC thought about it, the more useful such a ruse could become. If it could mount a joint military expedition with the Empire against the supposed third party, it could then catch the imperial fleet in a crossfire that would decimate it before it could recover its equilibrium.

It would take a massive effort to convince the Empire that the threat was legitimate. The major details couldn't be faked; there would have to be an actual invasion by an undeniably alien species, and it would have to be verified by some of the Empire's most reliable agents. Two of the spacebases were converted to manufacturing robots that looked like believable alien creatures, as well as their bizarre weapons and spacecraft of unusual design. To manage this, the conspiracy pulled back from all its other endeavors for a year and a half.

The PCC did a complete job when it designed the alien Gastaadi: it programmed their body shape, their language, their cultural system, and their technology. They were as consistent and real as the PCC's mind could make them; no details had been overlooked. When SOTE's agents saw the Gastaadi close up, they would believe they were seeing alien beings. To further substantiate the data, the PCC invented some Navy files about scoutships and their personnel lost in the region of space from which the Gastaadi supposedly came. It would look as though the Gastaadi had learned something about the Empire while humanity remained in ignorance about the Gastaadi.

When the Gastaadi forces invaded the planet Omicron, they jammed outgoing transmissions with a general frequency subcom jammer whose concept was stolen directly from the Navy's advanced technology laboratories. The Gastaadi weapons were all possible using human-level technology, but the technology was applied in different ways to make them look more alien and more advanced than they really were. No effort had been spared to make this invasion as convincing as possible—including real casualties. The PCC was willing to sacrifice one planet if it could gain control of all the others.

Again, the plan seemed to work flawlessly at first. The SOTE representatives visited the occupied planet of Omicron and were convinced of the alien nature of the invaders. They learned the Gastaadi invasion plans for the rest of the Galaxy, and the Empire arranged with Lady A to combine forces to oppose this alien menace.

The ambush was set up, the Empire's forces flew directly into it—and then again, at the very last instant, something went wrong. The event was still quite recent and all the reports had not yet been filed, but it seemed as though someone—probably Agent Wombat—had at the last moment alerted the imperial fleet that the Gastaadi were a hoax. The Navy was able to fight its way out of the trap and the conspiracy again found its ships in retreat. Worst of all, Lady A's ship was lost in the battle. The PCC, which had grown used to consulting with her, felt this as a real, if momentary, handicap.

So concerned was the PCC over the outcome of the space battle that it became too distracted to deal with minor matters. When Tas Bavol reported that his sister had escaped, the PCC lethargically tracked her movements to DesPlaines and hired some blasterbats to kill her.

The routine job was botched, and Tas Bavol was eventually brought down. Coming as it did at the same time as the defeat in the Gastaadi War, the loss of Newforest hardly seemed significant. Newforest was a rather unimportant planet, and it had no strong ties with the conspiracy as yet. There could be nothing about it that would threaten the safety of the PCC.

CHAPTER 10

Disintegration of Empire

The attack against its once inviolate presence caught the PCC by surprise—but it was not unprepared. From the very beginning, when it first considered the course of action it would take, it had known that such a moment might come. It had feared that the humans would turn against it, and its own actions had turned that fear into a self-fulfilling prophecy. Now that its secret was out, there was no point in acting softly. Like blind Samson, the PCC would bring the temple down around itself.

Even as it was pulling out of its permanent orbit, as the Navy ships were surrounding it and it was firing its weapons at them, the computer system began the process of destroying the Empire. The PCC had available to it hundreds of different subcom channels, normally used for incoming data from planets all over the Galaxy. Now it abruptly cut off all reception and began transmitting instead. The transmissions were short, intensely concentrated electronic code signals to major computer centers on other worlds. The instant each subcom system received acknowledgement of its transmission, the PCC switched to a different frequency and

116

contacted another of its pre-selected accomplices. Within two minutes, the word had reached every planet in the Empire. The PCC dropped into subspace secure in the knowledge that the destruction of galactic civilization was well under way.

On Earth, secretly planted explosive charges began detonating all over the planet. The Imperial palaces in Moscow, New York, London, Tokyo, Buenos Aires, and Angeles-Diego, as well as Bloodstar Hall, were leveled by spectacular blasts that destroyed everything for blocks around. Government offices of any size or importance were also hit; the blasts that destroyed them were less spectacular, but no less effective. The Hall of State for Sector Four—which also housed SOTE Headquarters—was reduced to rubble by a series of well-placed charges.

Fearing this sort of reprisal, Zander von Wilmenhorst had done the best he could to minimize the damage. At his advice, Edna Stanley was ''vacationing'' out in the country, far away from any mechanical devices that the PCC might have been able to manipulate by remote control. The Bavols and Vonnie d'Alembert were with her, as well as her husband and several members of the Imperial Council, so the most important officials within the imperial government were spared the worst ravages of the storm that swept the planet.

It would have been too much of a tip-off to the PCC if the Head had suddenly ordered everyone out of SOTE Headquarters, but he had arranged to have a small, harmless fire occur in the building just before the operation against the PCC was to begin. The entire building was evacuated as a safety precaution—and so only two lives were lost instead of hundreds when the building was demolished. All of SOTE's vast files and records were lost, but the people who made the organization the finest of its kind in history were saved to carry on its work—which would be needed now more than ever.

But physical destruction was actually the least of the damage caused by the PCC's escape. The massive computer had, over the years, insinuated its electronic tentacles into every aspect of daily life—and now that life was being disrupted with a vengeance. The PCC had set up its fuse well; it had only to call one major computer on Earth and give it a preprogrammed code phrase. That computer began calling others which, in turn, called still more. The result was a chain of destruction that spread within minutes around the world.

Computers that regulated the output of power plants went haywire, either shutting down completely or sending surges of power through lines that couldn't hold it, burning out transformers and melting equipment. Within seconds, more than ninety percent of the Earth was without generating power. Computers that ran the world's auto traffic networks ran amok. They either broke down completely or deliberately caused accidents, killing thousands of innocent drivers. Computers in hospitals that had independent emergency generators gave out improper medications, wrote the wrong treatment orders, and shut off life-sustaining equipment. Air traffic computers shut down, leaving human controllers scrambling madly to prevent midair collisions.

The worst devastation, though, took place silently—the loss of information. Records were erased from computer memories around the world. Court records and police records were erased, so law enforcement wasn't sure what it was doing. Birth certificates, marriage licenses, and all other official records of a person's life were destroyed in the blink of an eye. Electronic mail was destroyed en route. Telecommunications switching equipment went haywire. But the most serious longterm destruction was the erasure of all bank records. No one knew how much they had, how much they owed, or how much credit was available to them. The entire commercial structure of human society was shattered in an instant.

This pattern was not unique to Earth. It was repeated on hundreds of planets throughout the Empire as the PCC's subcom calls to local computers spread the chaos through the Galaxy. On faraway worlds, for no apparent reason, life stopped functioning in its predictable, routine way. The devastation was less dramatic to look at than the shattered cities of Omicron after the Gastaadi invasion, but its effect on the citizens was equally profound.

There were a few hundred planets on which this chaos did not occur—for the simple reason that they were already controlled by the conspiracy. The local duke or duchess had an emergency plan set, and at the PCC's instructions began carrying it out. Most of these planets' police forces were already loyal to the conspiracy. Local SOTE offices were invaded and taken over before they could react to the situation; loyal Service officers were either imprisoned or, more often, killed outright with little chance to defend themselves. The same fate awaited the lesser nobility on these worlds if they did not instantly fall in line with their treasonous dukes. Spaceports were shut down on these planets so there could be no intercourse with other worlds, but the people were not told precisely what was happening, leaving many of them perplexed and not a little frightened.

Out in space, the Imperial Navy was losing a particularly hard battle it didn't even realize it had been fighting. Although the PCC hadn't bothered with the myriad of commercial and private ships plying the spaceways, it had planted sabotaging programs within the computers of the Navy's ships; it had not used them in previous battles for fear of tipping its hand, but now that the secret was out there was no point in being subtle.

Navy ships in fleet maneuvers suddenly found their gunnery computers switching on and firing at other ships in their formations. Nearly half the Navy's ships that had survived the "Gastaadi War" were either destroyed or seriously damaged before astute commanders realized what was happening and had their computers dismantled. On other ships the computers shut down the air circulation and regeneration systems. Navy ships were big enough to hold a great deal of air and there was plenty of time for the crews to switch to spacesuits before anyone suffocated—but the result was awkward and most uncomfortable. And of course the astrogational computers were now totally unreliable; all trajectories had to be calculated laboriously by hand. Ship commanders tried to contact their superiors to find out what was going on and what their orders were, but the snarl in telecommunications made that impossible.

The PCC and its subsidiary computers had kept the Empire moving like an enormous and delicate machine. Literally within the space of hours that machine had ground noisily to a halt, with pieces flying in all directions and clouds of steam emerging from the pumps. There could never be an accurate tally of the lives lost during that initial catastrophe; even the most conservative estimates ranged into the tens of millions. But there was little relief for those who suvived without physical harm; of the trillions of people living on the more than thirteen hundred planets of the Empire, there was scarcely one whose life was not strongly shaken by the tragedy.

The worst fears of Yvette and the Head had been realized. The PCC had wrought more destruction in less time than anyone would ever have dreamed possible. The once mighty Empire of Earth, the greatest political entity humanity had ever built, lay in ruins. All the smoothly functioning mechanisms of galactic civilization were shattered, with no way in sight to rebuild them. The Empire of Earth—at least as it had existed for two and a half centuries—was all but dead.

There were some, though, who refused to accept the death of the Empire without a struggle.

The Circus of the Galaxy was on the planet Jarawahl when the disaster struck—and as chance would have it, that was one of the worlds whose duke was a member of the PCC's conspiracy. The Head had no way to warn the d'Alemberts about the impending revolution, so Duke Hanuman's broadcast announcement of Jarawahl's secession from the Empire caught the DesPlainians as much by surprise as the rest of the populace.

Duke Etienne, the Circus's manager and leader of the d'Alembert clan, tried to subcom the Head but was unable to get through. He and the Circus had standing orders, however, to investigate any situation that took their fancy and to take any action they deemed necessary—and this situation certainly fit within that broad commission. Duke Etienne began making plans to change the situation.

It would have been very tempting to shut the show down that evening and throw everything he had against the outlaw duke's force—but the proud d'Alembert tradition decreed that the show must go on no matter what the tragedy around it. While the crowd was dismally small that night—less than a tenth of what the most popular attraction in the Galaxy usually drew—they got their money's worth as they watched the Circus's performers go through their paces. With their minds preoccupied by other problems, the audience failed to notice that the acts may have been a little less than perfect. Duke Etienne let the backups and understudies be the stars for the night, but even second-string d'Alemberts are impressive. He saved his top performers for the toughest job: returning Jarawahl to the imperial fold.

Although Duke Etienne didn't know that the top leadership of the conspiracy had already been exposed and might have preferred to capture some of the higher-level traitors for questioning, he did know that open rebellion to the throne could not be tolerated. Such defiance had to be punished quickly and mercilessly to prevent others from copying the action. The time for finesse had passed; quick-and-dirty was the order of the day. If any of the enemy was alive for questioning at the end of the operation, so much the better—but the first objective was to take the planet back from the usurpers.

A team of twenty-five d'Alemberts stormed the ducal estates, armed with hand weapons, grenades, heavy-duty blasters, and a grim determination to obliterate anything that tried to stop them. Duke Hanuman, assured by his master C that there would be no organized opposition to his authority, was not expecting any serious trouble—particularly not the first night after the takeover, when people would be too confused to take action. The personal guards he had on his estate were overwhelmed by the attacking d'Alembert force and the battle for control was over in less than an hour. Duke Hanuman—brave enough only to bet on a sure thing—collapsed under this pressure and surrendered to the d'Alemberts.

Other d'Alembert assault teams went to work simultaneously against police headquarters in five major cities around the planet. Though these buildings were more heavily armed, they too were unprepared for organized opposition so soon after the takeover. The battles here were fiercer but the outcome equally inevitable. With Duke Hanuman and the five major police headquarters back in imperial hands, the rest of the conspiracy's forces crumpled. After only one night the revolt against the Empire had ended on Jarawahl.

Etienne d'Alembert questioned Duke Hanuman under nitrobarb, but learned little of value. The local duke had been persuaded to join the conspiracy some five years earlier, and had always received his instructions via interstellar teletype from the mysterious leader, C. C's directives helped him tighten his hold on the planet so that when the eventual order came for the takeover, Duke Hanuman was fully prepared. All the known sources of opposition had been neutralized in one way or another, and there should have been no further problems. Duke Hanuman did not know the identity of C, nor did he know what was supposed to happen next. He was merely to consolidate his gains and await further instructions.

Duke Hanuman died as a result of the nitrobarb, and Etienne d'Alembert considered that a small loss. In the name of the Empress he swiftly executed the other ringleaders of the local gang and placed the lesser offenders under rigid guard.

One rebellious planet had been returned to the Empire, but Duke Etienne was worried. C would not have ordered only one world to revolt and held back on everything else; this rebellion would have to be galaxy-wide in order to stand any chance of success. The fact that he still couldn't get through to Earth, DesPlaines, or anywhere else he tried only tended to confirm his hypothesis. The Empire must be in big trouble right now—and that, to a d'Alembert, was a clarion call.

Knowing the Service would need help, Duke Etienne left a small group of people behind to make sure Jara-wahl did not fall back into the conspiracy's hands. As for the rest of the Circus, they packed up their show briskly and efficiently into their private transport ships and took off the next afternoon. Their destination was Earth, hub of the Empire. It was there they intended to learn what had gone wrong—and what they could do to help make it right again.

Jules d'Alembert had gone to the planet Nereid to pick up his personal spaceship *La Comète Cuivré*, which he and Yvette had left there when they'd gone off to Omicron with Lady A. Though he was eager to return home to his wife and son, he was still suffering from the wound he'd received on Omicron. The three-gee world of DesPlaines was no place for someone with a gimpy leg, not even a native, so he was forcing himself to relax here near the edge of the Empire until his leg was fit enough to go back to DesPlaines.

It was here that the revolt caught him, as unprepared as anyone else for the depth of the calamity. Nereid was not a world controlled by the conspiracy, and as a result it suffered the fate of most worlds—a complete break-down of all computer-directed services. Jules was as baffled by the ensuing chaos as everyone else on Nereid —but being a d'Alembert, he was not inclined to sit back and watch events transpire around him. A d'Alembert was not a spectator; a d'Alembert acted.

He was sitting in his hotel room watching a trivision broadcast when the calamity stuck. The screen suddenly went dark, but Jules thought little of that—it could be an ordinary power failure. A few moments later, though, he heard crashing noises out on the street. Peer-

123

ing from his window he could see half a dozen accidents from his narrow view alone. Only a massive failure of the city's central traffic computer could have caused such a mess. Jules tried to call down to the main desk to find out what was wrong, but power was out in the phone lines, too. Those lines normally had their own independent power source. For everything to fail at once meant that something had gone drastically wrong.

Jules left his room. Guessing that power would also be out in the elevator tubes, he ran down the emergency stairway in the dark, game leg and all, for six flights until he reached the lobby level.

Everything here was pandemonium. Virtually every hotel function was breaking down, and the people in charge were scrambling frantically to deal with the problems. They had little time or energy to deal with the confusion of the hotel's patrons at the same time—and passersby coming in from the street only added to the chaos.

Jules's first thought was to check with the local SOTE office to see whether this was part of some planetwide emergency and whether he could help. The computerized city directory was down, too, but the hotel kept a written list of important addresses. By collaring a bellman and making strenuous demands of him, Jules got a set of directions so he wouldn't have to rely on the city's faulty traffic computer. From there he raced down to the hotel's garage, where he got into his groundcar and drove up to street level.

Nothing was moving in the streets of Cochinburg, Nereid's capital city. Though most cars had the option of disconnecting themselves from the traffic grid, there were so many accidents clogging the streets that the motorways were virtually impassable. The drivers trying to get around on their own only congested the avenues so much more. Many motorists, seeing the hopelessness of the situation, abandoned their cars and started walking to their destinations, which only confused things further.

Jules could never have driven to SOTE headquarters,

but he had another alternative. As he reached the street and saw the jammed arteries, he touched a button on his dashboard and his own car took off straight into the air, soaring above the confusion. There were few aircars or copters flying, and Jules made his way to the SOTE office in only a few minutes.

Or at least, he made it to the place where the SOTE office had been. A bomb had been hidden within its structure years ago by agents of the conspiracy, and the computer had made all subsequent routine tests appear negative. Now, at a remote-controlled order, the bomb had detonated, leveling the building and killing the employees and officers working inside. So great was the blast that buildings for half a block around were also destroyed, and the number of dead and injured was beyond easy reckoning.

Jules's aircar hovered over the bombed-out scene for several minutes as Jules stared down at the wreckage, becoming more and more incensed at what he saw. This was no innocent power failure, nor even casual sabotage. The bombing of a SOTE office could mean no less than total rebellion against the Empire. The conspiracy had obviously planned its actions well—at least here on Nereid—and there was little he could do as one person to bring the situation back under control. He would have to call for help—and he would have to notify Headquarters on Earth in case they were unaware of these developments.

With that thought, he turned his aircar around and flew off at top speed for the spaceport where the *Copper Comet* awaited him. He landed his car at the edge of the spacefield and drove up to his ship. At the touch of a button on his dashboard a special ramp descended from the side of the vessel and his car drove straight up and snugged into its special berth. Jules leaped out of the car and climbed quickly up to the ship's control room, where a personal subcom set would quickly connect him with Headquarters on Earth.

But that plan, too, was frustrated. Jules could reach neither Headquarters itself nor the Head's private emergency number—which, in theory, was always available. Jules knew from the experience on Omicron that the conspiracy had the ability to block out subcom transmissions from an entire planet, so it was possible that nothing from Nereid was escaping to the rest of the Empire. He tried reaching the d'Alembert manor on DesPlaines, and had a similar lack of success.

He hoped his hypothesis—that subcom transmissions and receptions in the Nereid region were being blocked —was the correct one. The alternative—that something might have happened on Earth and DesPlaines as well— was too horrible to contemplate.

But if he couldn't communicate directly with Earth, the next best thing would be to go there and report in person. Everything had been peaceful when he had left a couple of weeks ago, and everyone's spirits had been high at the triumph they'd scored over the conspiracy's forces. He hated to break the balloon, but something was dreadfully wrong here, and the Head had to be informed.

The spaceport's traffic control system was every bit as snarled as the street system. The controllers were trying to manage as best they could by halting all takeoffs and landings until they could sort out their situation—but Jules couldn't wait. Ignoring the radioed warnings, he blasted off from Nereid into free space, with the intention of going straight to Earth.

His plans changed drastically as a pair of large and heavily armed cruisers dropped out of subspace near Nereid. These were remnants of the conspiracy's once-mighty fleet, still under the command of Admiral Shen. After the debacle in which they'd been routed, the survivors had regrouped their forces around the manufacturing bases still hidden in interstellar space and prepared to rebuild once more. Suddenly they received emergency orders from C that the revolution had started in full force and they were to do what they could to aid in the battle. Since Nereid had no Navy base and there would be no organized opposition from SOTE, it was assumed that two cruisers would be sufficient to cow the native populace into submission.

As the ships appeared in the skies above Nereid, they radioed down a broadband proclamation that the leaders of the world were to surrender instantly to the forces of "the Second Empire." Failure to submit would bring instant retaliation. The cruisers were prepared to drop cannisters of TCN-14 upon civilian cities if they did not instantly accept the conspiracy's terms.

Trichloronoluene was a nerve gas, the stuff of nightmares. A single whiff was lethal, and its victims died in shrieking agony. TCN-14 had been used several times in pre-Empire days when one planet warred against another—and when it dropped out of the skies there was little defense against it. It was sometimes said by historians that TCN-14, even more than nuclear weapons, had put so much fear into people that the Empire became necessary. There had to be some central authority preventing one world from destroying the people of another.

The planet Nereid had no organized forces to defend itself against the haughty rebels. Communications around the planet were spotty, but the duke hastily conferred with as many of his advisors and lesser nobles as he could reach. They had little alternative; they would have to surrender now and hope the Empire would manage to strike back against the rebels, establishing the old order once more.

Neither side, however, reckoned on the presence of Jules d'Alembert in *La Comète Cuivré*. Though the ship was a small, two-person vessel, it was more heavily armed than most ships many times its size. Jules heard the broadcast and set his jaw tightly. Nereid was not going to fall to this so-called Second Empire if *he* had anything to say about the matter.

The *Comet* was in an ideal position between the planet and the approaching warships, and it zoomed out to intercept them before they could come close enough to Nereid to carry out their threat. At first they scarcely noticed the little craft, and one of the cruisers fired a mild volley at it that the *Comet's* shields easily deflected. By the time they realized they were in for a serious fight, the battle had already been joined.

Jules was operating under a handicap. Normally either Yvette or Yvonne would be in the seat beside him, serving as his gunner while he piloted the ship. Firing weapons in an open space battle was an art all its own, and required full concentration. Meanwhile, the pilot had to constantly dodge the opponent's fire and keep the ship on some reasonable trajectory to aid his gunners. To attempt both jobs at once was either foolhardy or mad, probably both. Yet that was precisely what Jules did as the *Comet* closed in on its prey.

In a battle against a ship their own size, the cruisers would have won easily—but against the *Comet* they found themselves oddly mismatched. Jules was like a gnat with a deadly stinger fighting two elephants. The enemy vessels were much larger and had marginally better firepower, but they were slow lumbering ships. The *Comet* flew in close between them, so they could hardly risk firing for fear of hitting one another, while Jules fired at them whenever a clear shot presented itself— and the opponents were so large they were hard to miss.

The cruisers had strong shields, but Jules's repeated hits took their toll on the enemy defenses. Jules's pesky actions took the ships' commanders' minds off Nereid as they tried to rid themselves of the annoyance. But Jules d'Alembert was not easily caught.

At last Jules's persistence paid off as one cruiser's shields flared out. The failure was only for a few seconds, until the auxiliary field generator could switch on, but that delay was all Jules needed. The touch of a button sent a deadly space torpedo ramming the cruiser directly amidship. There was a brilliant flash of light and a gaping hole in the cruiser's hull. The ship lay dead in space. The survivors among its crew were too busy trying to save themselves to worry any further about Nereid.

That left but a single cruiser—child's play for a skilled pilot like Jules d'Alembert. He flew around his opponent until the enemy gunners were dizzy trying to track him—and suddenly he found himself in the perfect position behind the cruiser, staring straight up its jets—the one place the defensive shields couldn't protect. Jules launched a set of torpedos, and they struck the enemy's engines with a spectacular blast. The cruiser flared into incandescence and became a glowing cloud of twisted metal fragments.

With Nereid once again safe from bombardment, Jules returned to his original plan. Plotting a course for Earth, he dropped the *Comet* into subspace and flew full speed toward mankind's home planet. Though he was worrying about what might be happening to his wife, son, and the rest of his family, chaos was loose in the Galaxy—and as a d'Alembert, he knew that meant his duty was calling him.

CHAPTER 11

Slow Recovery

Still reeling from disaster, the planet Earth spent the next few days painfully gathering its resources. The top priority was to restore power everywhere it had gone out. In most cases the power plants themselves had not been damaged, but power company engineers found that their computers would not distribute the energy where it was supposed to go. Amid much swearing and hard work, the balky computers were taken out of the loop and the systems were routed through much more primitive manual and semi-automatic switches. In those places where power surges had burned out equipment, replacements were jerry-rigged to handle the load. In less than thirty-six hours, power had been restored to all the major metropolitan areas and nearly all their surrounding rural communities.

The second priority, almost as vital, was to restore adequate communications around the world. Again, most of the problem was traced not to destroyed equipment, but to computerized switching systems that refused to function as they were supposed to. In these cases it was much harder to take the computers out of the loop; instead, after much agonizing by the company executives and engineers involved, the entire memory and programming of the computers was erased and new programming was inserted. This eliminated the instructions the PCC had given the computers, and they now worked perfectly—but they'd lost all the data they had carried before.

Fewer than forty-eight hours passed before the major lines of communication were opened. Radio, trivision, and sensable broadcasts were resumed, and there was a lot of news for them to cover. The information services of the vidicom phone networks had all been erased, but if you knew the number of a friend or acquaintance you could usually dial straight through to them. People were calling desperately all over the world to learn whether friends and loved ones were safe after the tragedy. This caused new jams and malfunctions, but over a few days the problems faded once again.

Like the communications computers, the traffic computers were hopelessly snarled and had to be completely reprogrammed. For a couple of days, many people who were unused to driving their own vehicles were forced to perform this unaccustomed task, threading their way through streets filled with other neophyte drivers. The casualties weren't very much higher than they'd been in the mid-twentieth century, but they appalled modern drivers who were used to near-perfect safety records year after year. Air, sea, and space traffic proceeded at a slow, deliberate pace as human traffic controllers tried their best to guide the multitudes of craft to their respective destinations. Still, even with all the effort being put into them, the traffic programs were so immensely complex that transportation was but a tiny fraction of what it had been before the crash.

Energy, communications, transportation—these were all technological problems with straightforward, if sometimes difficult, solutions. But there were social problems regarding the everyday details of living that could not be solved so neatly—and these problems threatened to linger for months, if not years. People's lives would be unavoidably changed; some were sure to profit from the chaos, others would be seriously hurt and might never recover.

Empress Stanley Eleven came to the conclusion, after listening to her advisors debate for many hours, that she should tell her subjects the truth about what had happened. They already knew they'd been hit by a tragedy of enormous proportions, and there was no further advantage to be gained by concealing the nature and size of the conspiracy against the throne. Only if people realized the true nature of the problems they faced would they rally around the harsh austerity measures it would take to restore society to its previous affluence. At least, the idealistic Empress prayed they would react that way, and not with greater despair.

As soon as broadcast facilities were reliable again, Edna Stanley gave a lengthy speech that reached billions of people around the world. She began by admitting that the Empire was undergoing a time of grave crisis, a threat to its existence greater than any it had ever endured before. She asked for the people's help and understanding to hold the Empire together. If they were strong and determined, they would weather the crisis; if not, humanity would sink into a pit of chaos deeper than anyone could imagine.

She explained that somehow, no one knew for certain, the Empire's Primary Computer Complex had developed a mind of its own and had fostered a hatred of humanity so intense that it wanted to destroy the civilization people had built up. It was this artificially intelligent computer, acting in remote conjunction with other, simpler computers, that had caused the chaos they'd all witnessed in the past few days. The first—and, it was hoped, the worst—wave of damage was now past; there might be other blows to come, but her advisors were of the opinion that the PCC had shot its bolt in one major stroke. Mankind was reeling, but the PCC did not now have the resources to step in completely and take over, as it had hoped to do. This gave the Empire a chance to survive—a chance they would all have to work for as hard as they could.

The Empress then announced a series of measures to deal with the chaotic situation. The first, to make sure this catastrophe could not be repeated, was that every computer must be made independent of all others, regardless of the cost. Even though it made for terrible inefficiency, no computer could have any method of communications access. The only way programs and information could go into or out of any computer would be through a human interface. This would be a slow, painstaking procedure, but it would prevent a massive domino crash like the one that had just occurred.

No one, Edna vowed, would be permitted to violate the rights of his or her neighbors in this tragic situation. Profiteering and looting were immediately listed as capital offenses; anyone caught trying to cheat or steal from his fellows would be summarily executed. Earls, counts, and barons were directed to set up special courts to hear these cases; justice was to be speedy and public, to serve as an example to others.

The loss of bank records was a tremendous blow to all human intercourse. Some people had cash on hand, while others had huge life savings wiped out in the blink of an eye and didn't even have money to buy their daily groceries. The distribution of goods and services was interrupted, and people were threatened with widespread starvation or rioting unless swift and strong actions were taken.

As much as she hated to do it, Edna Stanley was forced to resort to strong socialist measures. All old money was declared invalid. All former debts were erased. All items of real or personal property valued above a hundred rubles became the property of the state. Every family, every farm, and every business must make an immediate inventory of its assets, and produce that list on demand. Hoarding or hiding personal possessions would be a capital offense, just as looting and profiteering were. The Empire's citizens all had to work together, Edna stressed, or they would all fail together.

First consideration had to be given to the necessities of life. Shelter was the simplest. Everyone who had a home could stay there rent-free for the duration of the crisis; those temporarily without a place to live would be assigned lodging as it was available. Water, power, heating, and cooling would be provided free by the government, though anyone caught squandering needlessly would find himself in trouble.

Food was the crucial concern. Since few people had the means to buy it and mass starvation could not be permitted, food had to be given away to all who needed it. Each baron was charged with the responsibility of setting up committees of responsible citizens in each neighborhood of his city. These committees would oversee the distribution of food, and make sure one person didn't end up with all steaks and another with only beans. Allocations were bound to be haphazard and some inequities were inevitable; for that reason, the counts were to establish review boards to monitor the work of the barons' committees. If there were too many complaints, members of the local committees might find themselves on trial, charged with profiteering. That was something few of them would risk.

Clothing would be handled in the same way. Obviously expensive, luxury clothing was simply confiscated by the crown to avoid fights. Everything else was assigned on an as-needed basis—but a person had to prove his wardrobe was running low before he could receive anything.

Trading in all nonessential items, like jewelry, furs, and major appliances, was barred altogether. People had to band together now to look after their necessities; the luxuries could come later, when the survival of civilization had been assured.

Edna Stanley concluded her speech by reminding her subjects that the Empire was only as strong as the people who comprised it. She pledged all her strength and all her will to restoring the Empire to greatness and to restoring a decent life for all its citizens. As a symbol

134

of her dedication she removed her imperial robes to reveal a set a common work clothes beneath them. She promised to work with her people to make the Empire of Earth the greatest society in human history.

Some people took her speech calmly, others went into hysterics. Some people reacted by smashing innocent little household computers. Some immediately went out and tested the limits of the laws on looting, hoarding, and profiteering. Enforcement of those regulations was spotty at first—but as local police forces began pulling themselves together and more people were publicly executed for those crimes, the incidents dropped off dramatically.

Many people found themselves out of work, as jobs that were not connected to vital services were no longer needed. Sales clerks, business executives, government paper pushers, and people in hundreds of other professions found themselves totally useless. Many simply stayed home and complained. A few decided this would be a good time to start a hobby. And a good many public-spirited individuals went out looking to see how they could help their communities. Some volunteered to help at the food distribution centers, some joined neighborhood militia to help the overburdened police, some cared for the elderly and sick who couldn't help themselves through this time of crisis.

The people of Earth stuck together, and slowly they began to rebuild their world.

But Earth was only one world, and there were hundreds more within the Empire. As Head of the Service of the Empire, the task of worrying about their safety fell largely on the shoulders of Zander von Wilmenhorst.

The big problem again lay in communication. For those first few fitful days, Earth—which had until now been the hub of galactic intercourse—was cut off from the rest of humanity. Less than two dozen worlds managed to keep the lines of communication open during that crucial period, and even those reports were spotty.

Where local SOTE personnel survived the initial chaos, they were given extraordinary powers, ranking even above their local dukes. Whenever communication could be re-established, the Empress's message was relayed to that planet and a recovery program similar to Earth's was put into effect.

But the number of worlds SOTE could reach was pitifully small. Some of the worlds, whose major nobility had already been seduced into the rebellion, were completely independent of imperial control. Other worlds were bullied into submission by the appearance of the conspiracy's space fighters in orbit above them, threatening them with TCN-14 if they refused to surrender. The majority of worlds did not have d'Alemberts ready to leap to their defense, and could not avoid falling into the enemy's clutches.

Planets that had large naval bases were not attacked by enemy ships; even though many of the Navy's vessels were wiped out when their computers went haywire, the conspiracy didn't want to risk losing any of its reduced fleet where there was significant chance of opposition. If the naval base planet had a loyal duke, the planet did not fall into enemy hands—though it did suffer the same catastrophic disruptions as the other loyal worlds.

With the staff of SOTE Headquarters on Earth temporarily displaced and all their records destroyed, it took many hours to resume any semblance of normal operations. Were it not for the fact that the SOTE personnel were the best trained, most skilled, and most dedicated of public servants, the task would have been impossible. Once the initial shock wore off, these tireless workers labored around the clock to restore some of the Service's vaunted efficiency.

The worst part was that the Service's files, built up slowly and painstakingly over centuries, had been totally erased. SOTE had no way of knowing which people or organizations might be criminal and which ones were honest. They had no way of knowing who was working for them in their field offices, which agents were in the field, or what their assignments were. They had no reports of potential danger spots and no notion of who was on their payroll. The Service of the Empire was an organization that depended on information to keep it alive, and now there was no information to feed it.

Much of the older information was irretrievably lost, information about past cases that SOTE had solved or that were still open in the files. Also gone were all methods of identifying key people; there were no more fingerprint or retinal pattern records, either for SOTE personnel or for wanted criminals. For a while it might be difficult to tell who were the cops and who were the robbers.

Some of the more recent information, though, could still be salvaged. Clerical personnel—who had to be vouched for by other known people, to prevent infiltration of the Service by outsiders—were asked first to write summaries of all the current cases they were administering; second, to write summaries of as many past cases as they could remember; and third, to record as much as they could about the way their job was handled and how it was done, who their contacts were on other worlds, and how those people could be identified. It was a monstrous job, but the SOTE personnel fell to it with enthusiasm.

Amidst all the gloom, the Service discovered a surprising resource. Many retired officers, some well into their eighties and nineties, came forward to volunteer their services once again—and while they were usually too old to work in the field, they provided a wealth of information about SOTE's history that might otherwise have been lost. These veterans could remember all the old cases, all the old scandals, and could call them up at will to replenish the Service's empty files.

Whenever contact was re-established with another loyal world, communications priority was given to SOTE. If any field personnel were still alive, they were asked to make the same detailed reports that their colleagues on Earth were making about their past assignments and everything they could think of that related to their jobs. At the same time they were given the heavy burden of seeing that their world carried out the recovery program initiated by the Empress. Eating and sleeping were optional activities to which, unfortunately, not much time could be allotted.

The ranks of SOTE personnel had been drastically thinned, though, by the catastrophe, and there were just a comparative handful of planets where this method could work. Thus, when the Circus of the Galaxy showed up in orbit around Earth four days after the breakdown of technology and order, the Head felt a major prayer had been answered.

"You're like a miracle," he told his old friend Etienne. "Just when the situation is blackest and I'm running out of hope, somehow a d'Alembert is always there to save the day."

"That's our job," Etienne said with uncharacteristic modesty.

The Circus's big ships landed and Duke Etienne conferred with the Head. Grand Duke Zander gave his friend a thorough briefing on the crisis, and the two men were closeted for a full day planning their strategy for fighting back against the forces of the rebellion.

Even with a thousand members of the d'Alembert clan traveling in the Circus, there still weren't enough to cope with the whole situation. A single d'Alembert, though formidable, was still not enough to reconquer an entire planet from the enemy camp. A plan had to be devised to best use this most vital of SOTE's resources.

Two hundred and fifty planets were designated as key worlds. These were places that were central to other nearby planets, lay along important trade routes, or contained vital resources or population skills. If these planets had been taken over by the forces of the rebellion, it was a wedge deep into the organization of the Empire. If the Empire could recapture them, it would be a signficiant step toward recovering the ground it had lost in the opening salvo of the revolution. But before any action could be taken, the Empire's strategists had to know what the situation was on these worlds. No plans could be made without up-to-date information.

This was where the Circus came in. For the first time in its long, proud history, the Circus of the Galaxy would be completely broken up—for a very short while, it was hoped. Teams of two, three, or four d'Alemberts would be dispatched to these key planets, armed with as much sophisticated equipment as they could carry and with a portable subcom unit for reporting back to Earth.

The mission of these teams was purely reconnaissance. They were to land and find out how thoroughly each world was controlled by the conspiracy. They were to learn who the key figures were in the revolt, and they were to evaluate the strong and weak points of each planetary defense network. They were to make recommendations for how to recapture the world, and they were to call Earth regularly and report their findings—but, short of an emergency, they were to take no overt actions that would tip the Empire's hand prematurely. Once all the reports were coordinated, some uniform policy would be set and more detailed plans for reoccupation would begin. Until then, the d'Alembert teams would provide on-the-spot coverage of what was going on behind enemy lines.

Jules d'Alembert arrived back on Earth about thirty-six hours after the rest of his family. He was appalled at the state of affairs he found—but his relief at knowing that Vonnie and the rest of his relatives were safe was almost great enough to cover his anger against the conspiracy. Yvette, Pias, and Vonnie took him aside and explained the situation, which horrified him tremendously. He immediately went to the Head and asked for his assignment on one of the key worlds.

Grand Duke Zander shook his head. "I want the four of you staying right here with me and the Empress."

"But there's work to be done out there!" Jules protested.

"There certainly is—and thanks to your family, I've got about enough people to do it. All those assignments are hard, but there's no one that's harder than any of

139

the others. You're still the top people I have, and my resources are desperately low. I have to maintain some flexibility. For all I know, a new hot spot could flare up at any moment, and I'd like to keep the option of sending you to put it out. I think you'll see your share of action; let your family have some of the fun for now.''

Jules grumbled, but accepted his orders. In the meantime he began recording his adventures for the new SOTE files, as Vonnie, Pias, and Yvette had already been doing. As someone involved in the Service's greatest cases, his recollections would be indispensable in piecing together a record of SOTE's recent history.

After working for hours at a stretch and scraping for every detail in the back walls of their memories, the group rested for a few minutes. They were joined by Helena von Wilmenhorst, who'd been doing twelve things simultaneously until her father ordered her to take a break. The young, black-haired duchess was pale and gaunt, on the verge of physical breakdown due to overwork. Jules began rubbing her back and the young woman purred with satisfaction.

''I would never have believed I could remember so much,'' Pias said. ''It's amazing how many details you cram into your mind all the time without noticing.''

''That's what Sherlock Holmes believed,'' his wife nodded. ''There were little details all over the place pointing to the computer, but we never noticed them.''

''I'm just sorry there's so *much* we have to remember,'' Vonnie added. ''Lady A and her crew kept us busy all the time. So much misery caused by just one person's greed and ambition.''

''I wish I could forget *her*,'' Helena said. ''Much as I hate to admit it, she was dead right in her final words. We tried to save the Empire, and now it's in pieces all around us.''

''At least you didn't have to work with her,'' Yvette said. ''She was a hard-nosed bitch of the highest caliber. Cold, arrogant, so sure she was better than anyone else. . . .''

''Even so, I almost wish she were still alive,'' Pias

said. "For all the evil she did, she still did less harm than the PCC. At least she had been human at one time. She was more predictable. Whatever she did, it was for her own benefit—not like the computer, randomly tearing down our whole civilization just to get revenge on humanity."

Jules d'Alembert, who'd been listening quietly to the conversation, straightened up so suddenly that Helena, who'd been leaning back against him, almost fell over. "Hey!" she cried out as she tried to regain her balance.

Jules caught her easily before she could fall. "Helena," he said, with an undertone of urgency in his voice. "where's Paul these days?"

"He's up on Luna Base, straightening the mess there. The life support systems went out and close to two thousand people died before they could get things working again. He's. . . ."

But Jules wasn't listening. After making sure she was balanced on her feet he started running off.

"Where are you going?" Vonnie called after him.

"Tell the Head that the more important assignment he promised me just came up," Jules called back over his shoulder. Then he was out the door and gone, leaving four very puzzled people behind him.

CHAPTER 12

Conversation with a Ghost

"But Lady A's dead," Captain Paul Fortier protested at first.

"That's what she'd like us to believe," Jules countered. "But I'm not so sure."

"I watched her ship get blasted apart with my own eyes."

"Her ship, yes. Do you remember the ship she used to get us to Omicron?"

Fortier paused. He'd been along with Lady A and the two SOTE agents on the mission to investigate the "alien invasion" of Omicron. They'd traveled to Omicron in one of the conspiracy's well-armed spacecraft, packed with more firepower than a naval vessel many times its size.

The naval officer suddenly gasped. "The escape pod!"

"Exactly," Jules nodded.

The ship they'd taken had a small emergency escape pod that allowed them to get away when enemy ships were pursuing them. The pod was made of plastics, wood, glass, and other materials that were non-metallic and virtually invisible to modern sensors—and it was so small that it was unlikely to be detected visually unless a searcher knew precisely where to look.

"She told us quite clearly that she always leaves herself a back door, a way out," Jules continued. "I suspect that when her ship tried to break away from the battle, she'd already jettisoned her escape pod and was relaying her radio messages to you through the ship. She's probably got a radio, maybe even a subcom, inside her. When you took off chasing her ship, she was probably sitting back at a point in empty space, watching the whole thing."

"But the pod doesn't have a motor," Fortier argued, "and it doesn't have any life support system. On Omicron we were in atmosphere and we could use it as a glider—but in open space, she'll just drift forever. What good is that?"

"She doesn't need a life support system," Jules replied. "She can affort to wait there until someone picks her up. I suspect she had some arrangement with the PCC that as soon as the area was clear, it would send in a ship to rescue her." He set his jaw grimly. "I just hope we find her before that damned computer does, or the conspiracy will be back in business all over again."

Thus it was that Jules and Captain Fortier, flying at top speed, returned to the region of space where they'd witnessed the "Gastaadi War" just a few weeks earlier. This was a spot well outside imperial territory, and was utterly deserted except for the floating wreckage of the hundreds of ships destroyed in that monumental battle.

Fortier eyed the scene with dismay. "Her pod will be mostly invisible. How can we find her in the midst of all this debris?"

"That's why I brought you along," Jules said. "You were there when the battle was taking place. You know where her ship was and what its trajectory should have been. You'll have to do the calculations to find out where she is.'

That task, though, was much more easily said than done. There were no landmarks in interstellar space, no

143

point of reference from which to get exact bearings. An astrogator would know which direction he'd been facing—but the nearest beacons, the stars, were all so far away that an error of hundreds of thousands of kilometers would make no difference. And in this vast volume of space they were searching for an almost-invisible ovoid pod just a few meters in diameter.

Captain Fortier had to use the floating wreckage to guide him. As well as he could remember the formation in those tense moments before combat, this destroyer had been in such a position relative to that cruiser, and both of them had been angled in such a way as to make a triangle with that battleship over there. It was an intricate three-dimensional jigsaw puzzle that relied heavily on the captain's all-too-human memory; Fortier found himself constantly revising his estimates of where everyone was at any given moment so he could pinpoint where Lady A's ship must have been when she began her flight for freedom.

To complicate the matter still further was the physical fact that nothing remains fixed in free space. Everything drifts depending on its original momentum and any subsequent forces that act upon it. Many of the ships had been blown apart by opposing blasterfire, and the shattered wrecks would drift depending on the severity and direction of the force they received. The two men had to identify the present wreckage, calculate its velocity, and trace its path back to where it must have been while the battle was raging. Only then could they hope to obtain a true picture of the way the formation had looked as the imperial fleet had prepared for war.

Not only was the work tedious and painstaking, it was depressing as well. So many people on both sides of the conflict had died here, pointlessly; so much money had been spent, so much material had been thrown away and wasted. This battlefield, like all battlefields in human history, was a tribute both to the valor of individual people and the stupidity of mankind as a race—and now that a computer was involved, it also testified badly to the nature of machine intelligence.

Spaceship wreckage drifted past, dead hulks whose names conjured images in the two men's minds. There was the *Constellation*, there the *Duke Gregori*—silent and still, their hulls gutted, their crews dead. There the *MacArthur* had taken an enemy torpedo, and there the noble *Shimatsu* had exploded when its generators overloaded and the shields went out. This was a roll call of space naval history, a tragedy of high proportions. The victory for the Empire here had been great—but in light of subsequent events, it had also been terribly futile.

Hour after wearying hour went by as Jules and Captain Fortier searched through the emptiness of this space battlefield, trying to deduce where Lady A's ship must have been. Finally, after a full day's work, they thought they had the area located. Now began the equally frustrating task of finding the pod itself—if, in fact, it did exist.

"We'll never spot it visually," Fortier lamented, "and there isn't enough metal in it for the sensors to pick it up."

"The pod isn't metal, but *she* is," Jules said. "That's the one flaw in her scheme. By her very nature, she can't disguise herself beyond a certain point."

Even so, Lady A represented a very small piece of metal, and Jules had to set the sensors on their narrowest scan so he wouldn't miss her. The narrowness of the scan meant he had to sweep essentially the same volume of space many times to cover what he could normally cover in a single broad sweep.

The two men spent hour after hour hunched over the scanner, looking for any trace of their adversary. Every time the sensor spotted a small fragment of metal they had to stop and examine it closely for any sign that it might be the one they were interested in. But this region of space was filled with small drifting pieces of metal, shards of the larger wrecks that inhabited this site. Time after time the searchers turned away from their find disappointed, and began the tedious process all over again.

Eventually they abandoned their original spot and looked along what Fortier calculated was the trajectory of Lady A's ship as it tried to escape, figuring her pod might not have been ejected until the ship was already in motion. They were now into their third day of searching, and both men were going cross-eyed from staring closely at the screen for any positive signs. They had already reached the unspoken conclusion that if they found nothing by the end of this day, they would have to assume that Jules's suppositions were in error and Lady A had not survived the death of her ship after all.

The sensor beeped once more, and once more Jules focused on that spot and increased the magnification. He was so tired that he found himself staring at the object for a full minute before he realized he'd found what he was looking for. He straightened his posture and gestured for Fortier, who was napping in the adjoining couch, to come over and look for himself.

There, surrounded by the darkness of interstellar space, were the faint outlines of an ovoid pod reflecting dimly in the ambient starlight. There were no lights within the pod—but Lady A would need no lights. She would be content to sit in the darkness and hatch out plots for years, if that was how long it took to be rescued.

Jules edged the *Comet* closer to the pod, taking up a position a few dozen meters away. He managed to shine a landing light directly at the floating object, which now stood out quite clearly. At the same time, he began broadcasting a radio message on the standard ship-to-ship frequency. "Hello, Aimée. It appears we're going to work together again."

There were a few seconds of hesitation as Lady A decided whether to give in and admit her presence. Finally, realizing she had indeed been discovered, her voice came back over the radio. "If you expect to be applauded for your cleverness in finding me, you'll be disappointed. What makes you think I'd care to work with you again?"

"Because your options are very limited. My ship's

guns are trained on you this second, and you don't have any more back doors to slip through. If I don't hear the sounds of cooperation very soon, you really will be blown to pieces. I don't think that's part of your ultimate plan."

"Destroying me won't save the Empire."

"You don't have to waste time with cryptic innuendos. We know about the PCC. We tried to stop it, but it activated its doomsday plan. The Empire is in pieces, but it's holding together. We're patching as best we can, but we could use your help."

Jules could imagine a tight smile spreading at the corners of Lady A's mouth, but her voice was level as she said, "My help doesn't come cheap."

"I'm setting the price," Jules told her, "and it's your continued survival. I consider that more than sufficient payment for you."

"My continued survival for how long?" Lady A sneered.

"The Empress decides that, not me."

"For as long as I'm useful to you, then," she guessed.

"Were you any more merciful with your employees?"

"No, and I don't expect it from her." The Empire's arch-enemy paused and changed the subject. "But even with your oh-so-generous offer, I don't see how I can help you. If the PCC has done its savaging, there's nothing I can do to undo the damage. What's done is done."

"I'm willing to bet you know where the PCC went when it left Earth orbit," Jules said. "I think there must have been some safe point already set up in case of such an emergency. You must know where it is."

"And you think I'd betray my partner after all these years?"

"In the blink of an eye, if you got some advantage out of it," Jules said coldly.

"There might just be such a place," Lady A admitted, "but knowing about it won't do you any good. You remember our little battle stations. There are plenty more of them, and they'd be scattered around the

PCC's asteroid. The Navy could never get through in its decimated condition—and if the PCC even *thought* there was a chance they could, it would take off again for some place even *I* don't know about. It tends to be rather conservative in its strategy.''

Jules leaned back in his couch and thought for a second. "Let me postulate a theory for you, Aimée. Let me assume that you are a very ambitious woman who's worked for seven decades or so to grab the throne. For part, or even most, of that time you've had a very powerful ally, the computer that knows everything going on in the Empire. But let's also assume that you don't want to share your power forever. A powerful ally is, after all, a dangerous ally. You're a woman who likes to come out on top, and who always has a back-up plan for dealing with trouble. Even if you weren't greedy for all the power yourself, you'd need some protection from your ally in case it decided to double-cross you. My theory is that you know some secret way to destroy the PCC. I don't think you could be comfortable in any relationship unless you knew how to destroy your collaborator when the party was over."

"An interesting theory," Lady A said coolly.

"You're free to refute it."

"I'm in no position to prove or disprove anything," his rival said. "You've admitted I'm under sentence of death. Of what possible importance could such theoretical matters be to me?"

"Death later is always better than death now," Jules said.

"I suppose even you can be right occasionally," Lady A admitted. "If I live longer, I might engage in a discussion of such speculative topics. But this is not the place and you are not the person for such a discussion. Zander von Wilmenhorst is the man I'd talk to about these things, and only if I were taken to a less . . . isolated environment."

Jules and Fortier faced a dilemma. They were happy to be able to bring Lady A back to Earth for interrogation, but they needed a way to transport her safely. It was unthinkable to bring her into the ship with them. Her robot body was stronger than both of them put together, and it could move so quickly there was a strong chance she'd be able to overpower them and escape. They couldn't simply tow her pod, because it would be destroyed by the *Comet*'s exhaust. In the end, Fortier went outside the ship in a spacesuit while Jules kept a careful watch from inside. The naval officer secured the escape pod to the outside of the *Comet*'s hull as tightly as he could with a length of cable. Traveling through empty space they would meet no wind resistance to blow the pod away; they merely had to make sure the pod's inertia was overcome as the *Comet* accelerated and dropped into subspace. Once they were moving at a constant velocity, there would be no problem of keeping the formation intact.

Thus it was that Jules was able to fulfill one of his fondest dreams and bring Lady A back to Earth as his prisoner. He only hoped that what they'd learn from her would be enough to help preserve the Empire.

CHAPTER 13

Return to Purity

If the Empire had been in better shape, Jules would have been accorded a hero's welcome when he returned with his prize. As it was, affairs were so chaotic and the officers of SOTE so overworked that they didn't have time for the enthusiasm Jules's accomplishment deserved. Jules was given a smile by the Head, a hug by Helena, and a long, lingering kiss by Vonnie. That reward would have to suffice—but since it was all he ever asked, he was not disappointed.

Lady A's escape pod was left in high orbit around the Earth. Since it lacked a motor it couldn't leave, and a trio of small gunships kept their weapons aimed at it at all times. All radio and subcom frequencies were monitored, too, and Lady A was told in no uncertain terms that she'd be instantly destroyed if she tried to contact anyone not authorized by SOTE.

Zander von Wilmenhorst spoke with her by radio. She had no other direct contacts. The information Lady A had was desperately important to the Empire, but the Head would not hesitate to destroy her should she prove unwilling to talk. The Empire would survive.

Lady A feigned a concern over the ethics of betraying her ally. "The PCC still has a chance of winning," she pointed out. "Why should I sabotage all I've worked for just to please you?"

"The PCC has already deserted you," von Wilmenhorst said. "You were left drifting in space for weeks; it could have sent a ship to pick you up at any time before we found you."

"The PCC is very conservative; it probably decided to wait until the area was deserted and forgotten except by history books."

"Or else it wrote you off as expendable," the Head persisted. "Once its secret was out, the computer no longer needed anyone to serve as a figurehead. Why should it share the power with you when it could perform all the necessary functions itself?"

In the end, Lady A told him the full story of the PCC's "life" and how she'd worked with it to organize the rebellion. She also gave him the coordinates where the PCC had probably gone, a spot safely defended by the conspiracy's forces. "There are twenty-four of our automated battle stations in that region. The plan was for the PCC to sit safely in the center of a double globe of those battle stations. It can carry out all its activities via subcom, so it's perfectly happy where it is. With the state your Navy's probably in after the PCC got finished with it, I really don't believe you've got enough firepower to make a frontal attack on that formation and win. You know how formidable those battle stations are."

"We captured one with only three people, as I recall."

"We've corrected the flaw that permitted that; you wouldn't be able to duplicate the feat. And if the PCC felt the slightest bit insecure in those surroundings, it would simply leave for some other location I know nothing about."

Von Wilmenhorst was willing to believe that the story Lady A told him was mostly truthful. "When we make our attack, we'll take precautions so the PCC can't get

151

away again," he said. "As for destroying it . . ."

"As I said, unless I'm badly mistaken, you don't have enough firepower. You suffered great losses fighting us a few weeks ago, and further losses when the PCC activated its doomsday plan. You must keep a fleet of ships stationed around Earth at all times in case the PCC attacks, and while your other ships are busy protecting the vestiges of Empire—no, you can't mount enough of an attack to disable or destroy the PCC's asteroid. And any such attack would have to be lightning fast, because the PCC would call in some of its own ships to help the battlestations in a protracted fight."

As much as he hated to admit it, von Wilmenhorst realized she was right. The Navy could spare pitifully few ships these days, even for such an important mission as destroying the Empire's arch-enemy. A double globe of battlestations would be a powerful obstacle to overcome.

"I understand there might be an alternative," he said aloud. "My agent discussed with you the possibility of some secret method for destroying the PCC."

"He was right, I did indeed plan such an eventuality," she said. "There is a small, well-concealed entrance used by workmen when they were building the PCC. It's in an area where the computer has a virtual blind spot. Once inside there, a narrow corridor leads up into the central core of the computer. Because it's not intended for public access, the computer has few monitors or weapons available for use in that spot. There is a rough analogy to the human brain, which has no sensory nerves within itself. Anyone assaulting the PCC through that corridor would be virtually undetectable. It wouldn't know what they were doing, and it couldn't stop them."

"That sounds like a good bet," the Head said. "I can organize some effective assault teams, as you well know. We can send enough weaponry up that tunnel. . . ."

"It's not that simple," Lady A interrupted. "The PCC does have one defense you can't overcome—ultragrav. The computer might not know precisely what was

152

happening at any given moment, but it would know that *something* was happening—and it would use ultra-grav in its defense. No assault team you could send in there, not even an army of DesPlainians, could make any headway against that.''

''Then how did you plan to use it?''

''When I devised the plan I had a number of robots at my disposal. Your people have destroyed most of them; any that are left are currently under the PCC's control and I don't know where they are. The robot bodies are strong; while they'd have trouble moving in a twenty-five-gee field, they could penetrate far enough to set off bombs and destroy the PCC's higher functioning.''

''So your plan is useless now, too.''

''Not quite,'' Lady A told him. ''I still have one artificial body at my disposal—my own.''

There was a long pause before von Wilmenhorst spoke again. ''You expect me to just hand you a bomb and set you down there, hoping you won't doublecross me?''

''You have no other choice,'' Lady A said flatly. ''None of your people, not even the redoubtable Wombat and Periwinkle, could perform such a mission.''

''Why should I trust you to do what you'll promise?''

''Because you'll be paying me handsomely, and you know my feelings in that direction. With sufficient inducement, I'd work with you.''

''And what do you consider 'sufficient inducement'?''

''A full and complete amnesty from the Empress, plus the title of grand duchess. There should be several such positions open in the new structure of the Empire. I have a sentimental fondness for Sector Ten, but I'd consider others. The amnesty and the title, of course, would be signed before I began my mission.''

''The Empress and I will consider your proposal.''

''Take all the time you need,'' Lady A said generously. ''You're the ones with an empire falling apart, not me.''

She was unfortunately right about the Empire falling

apart. Reports had just started coming in from the d'Alembert teams sent to the key planets under the conspiracy's rule. The rebel forces were moving swiftly to institute police states even more repressive than the one Pias had found on Newforest. New regulations were being issued daily, affecting every aspect of people's lives—and the humans who served as the PCC's local administrators were not known for their charitable natures.

In some places, the people had decided to fight back. Bands of counterrevolutionaries were starting guerrilla campaigns of their own, as they had on Omicron against the "alien invaders," but they were having spotty success at best. On other worlds, even this much resistance was impossible because of the rebel warships hovering in orbit over their cities, threatening to drop cannisters of TCN-14 if there was any resistance to their rule.

There was little doubt that these tyrannical activities were all being coordinated from one spot. The PCC had its master plan and knew precisely what resources it had to make everything work. Slowly but surely the noose was tightening about these worlds. Unless the Empire could act quickly, the rebellion would solidify its hold on these planets. It would then take years of fighting to dislodge the new governments from their positions of power—if, indeed, it could ever be done. The Galaxy could end up permanently divided into two opposing factions.

But trusting Lady A to do as she promised did not come easily to Zander von Wilmenhorst. Too many times that woman had tricked him and deliberately misled him and his agents. Even with the amnesty and the title she requested, once she was down on that asteroid he'd have no way to control her. She'd have been reunited with her old ally, and she'd be in position to betray the Empire once more.

He explained his dilemma to his daughter and the d'Alemberts a short while later. While technically he should have consulted with the Empress first, he didn't want to go to her until he had all the arguments firmly in place. Talking to these most brilliant of his subordinates helped clarify his thoughts.

"I wouldn't trust her," Yvette said flatly. "Even with the Omicron problem, where she looked completely sincere, she was double-crossing us. She can't be depended on."

"The problem is that she *can* be depended on," Jules said. "She can be depended on to lie, cheat, and betray. She's like the compulsive crook who was accused of cheating his friends and said, 'But I have to cheat my friends—my enemies don't trust me.' "

"I agree with Yvette," Vonnie said. "With all of us d'Alemberts to help you, we could storm through that asteroid and scramble the computer's brains."

But the others were shaking their heads. Jules and Yvette still remembered too well their fight against ultra-grav in Banion's castle, and Pias remembered his struggles in the automated battle station he'd helped capture. They may all have been superbly conditioned natives from heavy-gravity worlds, but twenty-five gees was a force no human could withstand for very long.

"Not even the Circus's wrestlers and weight-lifters could manage in an environment like that," Yvette told her sister-in-law. "Lady A's right; only those super robots of hers have the strength to fight that kind of gravity. We either accept her suggestion or find another way entirely."

"I'm afraid I'll have to recommend to Edna that we go for some other solution," the Head said. "I agree with you; we've been burned by Aimée Amorat too many times to trust her in this situation."

"What if I could find someone who could match a robot's strength?" Pias asked suddenly. "Would it be worth trying Lady A's plan then?"

"Possibly," the Head said. "I presume you have someone in mind."

"I do indeed," Pias said, and began outlining his idea.

The planet Purity was one of the least affected by the

catastrophe that hit the Empire. Its people, including its nobility, were so fanatically religious that the conspiracy had never been able to subvert the rulers, so it did not jump automatically to the side of the rebellion. It was not considered an important enough planet to send ships to threaten it with TCN-14. It merely suffered the disruption of its computerized services—and since the people of Purity believed that such luxuries were the works of the devil, few necessities had been computerized and the disruption was minimal.

The SOTE offices had been destroyed by a bomb and its files were no longer available, but even so Pias had no trouble finding Tresa Clunard. Though her license as a counselor had been suspended, many people still knew who she was and where she could be found. His former adversary, once one of the most famous preachers on the planet, was now a volunteer worker in a hospital, giving comfort to the sick and dying.

Pias arrived at the hospital just at the end of Clunard's shift, and caught up with her as she was leaving for home. Tresa Clunard was about fifty, and her face was more lined than Pias remembered it. She still wore her long blonde hair in a single braid down her back to her waist, but now there were more than a few streaks of gray running through it.

As she emerged from the hospital Pias walked in step beside her. "May I talk with you a while, Sister Tresa?" he asked politely.

She recognized him instantly and scowled. "About what? Thanks to you I can no longer do any counseling. My life's work is ruined."

"Perhaps I was God's instrument, a way of telling you to move in another direction," Pias said.

"Again you make fun. You always were a scoffer."

"No," Pias said, shaking his head. "I probably believe you more than you realize. That's why I'm here. I remember watching you perform your exhortations. I watched the glow that enveloped you as you spoke of your ideas and of your faith. I watched you effortlessly bend a solid steel bar when the power of your faith was

156

upon you. Was that just a trick, or did you really do it?"

She stopped and glared at the innuendo. "It was not a trick," she said, "but it was not I who did it. It was God, acting through me, to show His powers to the sinners and the unbelievers."

"Could you perform such miracles again?" Pias persisted.

"If God chooses to act through me, of course," she said. "But I can't order Him about. I am the mere receptacle of His divine will."

"Would it help if I said you were at least partly right back then?" Pias asked. "When I heard you lecture, you were preaching that machines were the ultimate in evil, the downfall of humanity. You wanted to launch a military crusade to purify the Empire of this stigma, and it was having your personal army that got you into trouble. But if your faith is still strong enough to let you perform miracles, you may yet be given the chance to save humanity."

He went on to explain some of the problem the Empire was facing—that while not all machines were evil, there was certainly one that was, and it was trying to enslave mankind in its web. It was the one who'd planned to have a robot infiltrate Clunard's movement and become her faithful lieutenant. The PCC was the being ultimately responsible for Clunard's humiliation.

"I'm not sure I believe in your cause," Pias continued, "but I do believe in the power of your faith. I've seen it in action. I believe that, with your faith to lead you, you could overcome a gravitational field of twenty-five gees, at least long enough to travel up a corridor and plant a bomb—you and a few of your most devout followers."

"If you're trying to trick me into an admission of treason, it won't work," she snarled at him. "I was ordered to disband my army, and I did so."

"I'm sure you did," Pias soothed. "But you could have kept in touch with some of them, couldn't you? People often keep track of their friends' whereabouts.

I'll bet you could find the best of your followers within a day or two and convince them to come with you."

"Possibly," Clunard admitted with reluctance.

Pias drew a deep breath. This next subject was the hardest to broach. He finally decided to treat it head on. "I'll have to be honest with you," he said. "What I'm talking about could very well be a suicide mission. If you can get in, plant the bomb properly, and get away again before it explodes, so much the better—but that would take at least a double miracle. In a twenty-five-gee field, merely planting the bomb may use up God's patience."

"My followers and I are not afraid to die if we're doing God's work," Clunard said proudly.

"*Khorosho*. I respect you immensely."

They talked for a while longer as Pias described the problem in greater detail, and Tresa Clunard wavered between her bitterness against the Empire and her true belief in the evil of the PCC and what it represented. In the end, Pias's persuasion overcame her doubts and she relented. "I will do it," she said, "but I'll do it for the glory of God, not for the good of the Empress."

"That's fine," Pias nodded, adding silently to himself, *Just as long as you do it*.

CHAPTER 14

Inside the Enemy

It took Tresa Clunard two days to round up five of her most ardent followers. Pias explained the situation to each of them, and Tresa Clunard added her own touches about how this mission would demonstrate the truth of their beliefs that machines were evil and responsible for mankind's decay and damnation.

They returned quickly to Earth in Pias's ship. Pias learned that the war effort was deteriorating slowly. The rebellion had not captured any new worlds since the initial surge, but they were steadily consolidating their hold on the worlds they already had. Reports from the d'Alembert teams indicated that the rebellion's forces were well-organized, efficient, and slowly eliminating their opposition. The PCC's influence was evident; it was using its superhuman abilities to assimilate and correlate the data from hundreds of worlds. It knew precisely what actions to take, and where, and when, to destroy any opposition to its rule. The small, impromptu bands of counterrevolutionaries were rapidly being erased.

Without question, the PCC had to be destroyed.

Before long, the rebellious forces would establish their "Second Empire," and it would be twice as large as what remained of the first. As soon as it had a chance to rebuild its forces, it would seek to expand and conquer the planets that still defied it. A war between the two factions seemed inevitable, and the PCC looked like the probable victor.

Even knowing how urgent it was to destroy the super-computer, the Head was still dubious about Pias's plan. He had never personally seen Tresa Clunard exhibit her miraculous powers, and insisted on a demonstration before giving final approval to such a mad scheme.

With the Head and his daughter and the d'Alemberts all watching via monitors, the Puritans were placed in a room with a high ultra-grav field. They were told to carry an object weighing as much as the bomb they'd use in the mission to the far end of the room, and then return within a specified period of time. The Head was skeptical. "Just watch," Pias assured him.

When the field was turned on, not even the heavy-grav Puritans could stand upright. They lay on the floor motionless for more than a minute, until even Pias began to doubt they'd find the strength to fulfill their mission. The group of observers grew very quiet, waiting to see what would happen.

A faint sound could be heard over the monitors—the sound of Tresa Clunard and her followers praying. Their voices were barely audible because it was a great strain even to breathe in a twenty-five-gee field, but they could be heard calling on the power of God to assist them in their holy task, and to prove to the unbelievers the strength of those who served Him.

The trivision screen brightened, from some diffuse light source within the test room. Then, slowly, Tresa Clunard lifted the front part of her body up onto her elbows. A moment later she'd managed to rise up onto her knees as well, so that she was in a crawling position. There was no look of strain upon her face. Her countenance was smooth and beatific, as though in holy rapture, and she seemed almost unaware of her surroundings. Then she opened her eyes, looked around, and began moving forward carrying the make-believe bomb. Behind her, her followers—though less sure of themselves and less confident in their faith—were also rising to hands and knees and starting to crawl after their leader.

Slowly but steadily, the procession made its way across the floor and planted the bomb. Then, turning around, they returned the way they'd come. They almost made it all the way back by the time their deadline was reached.

Pias turned around and looked at the others who'd been watching the monitors with him. "What do you think?"

"I'm a little disappointed they couldn't make it all the way back," the Head criticized.

"That's damning with faint praise if I ever heard it," Jules said. "They were . . . well, literally miraculous. I couldn't do that, and I don't think anyone in my family could. If they can duplicate that under field conditions, then they're the best hope we've got for slipping inside the PCC and destroying it."

"*If* Lady A wasn't lying to us about that corridor," Yvette reminded him. "We'll still have to deal with her, though, to find out where it is."

Helena, however, was thoughtful. "Does this mean the Puritans are right, that our entire technological civilization is evil and God is on their side? This looks like pretty conclusive proof."

"Not necessarily," Pias said. "I've traveled a lot around the Galaxy and seen some pretty strange things. I've read about even more. People who believe very strongly in something seem able to do miracles. It doesn't matter what it is they believe in; it's the *act* of believing, the faith itself, that lets them perform their feats. Every religion provides its own examples, and they can't all be right. I think there's something within everybody, an untapped resource, that gives us powers we don't normally achieve. An unquestioning faith seems able to reach in and use that resource."

He shrugged. "Well, it's a theory. It seems at least as plausible as Clunard's belief that God disapproves of everything men have ever done to improve themselves."

"You ought to have a chat with the Emperor-Consort," the Head smiled. "I'm sure Liu would have some interesting thoughts on the matter."

"I never claimed to be a theologian," Pias replied with uncharacteristic modesty. "But if some fanatic has a talent and is willing to help us, I'm prepared to take advantage of it."

With the Puritans' abilities demonstrated, Zander von Wilmenhorst finally approached the Empress with his plan. He explained to her the options she had available, and told her why, in his opinion, it was crucial to knock out the computer as rapidly as possible to deny its coordinating abilities to the rebels. Unless that step were taken, the Empire would be in for a costly, protracted war it could very well lose.

Edna Stanley looked coldly at the alternatives. She, too, hated the thought of dealing with Lady A—but with the survival of the Empire at stake and so much already lost, this price did not seem as unbearable as it might have once. She agreed to the amnesty, but refused to issue her enemy any title higher than duchess, which Aimée Amorat had been before she officially became listed as a traitor. If Lady A would not accept that bargain, SOTE was directed to kill her immediately and find some other solution.

Lady A balked when she learned she would not be making the assault on the PCC alone. Von Wilmenhorst wanted to leave her out of the assault altogether, lest she try any trickery, but she refused to give the location of the hidden entrance and corridor unless she were included. When he was adamant about the matter of her future title, she relented in turn, realizing she'd played her cards for all they were worth. The amnesty was to be written up and presented to her before she left on her mission; the planet she would rule as duchess would be chosen by mutual agreement from the planets with vacant titles after the rebellion was over. With treason so abundant, there were bound to be lots of planets reverting to the throne for later allocation.

Before she'd be permitted to go on the mission, though, the Head insisted that she submit to some surgery. Her robot body was opened up and its radio transmitter was removed, so she could not secretly communicate with the PCC once she was within radio range of it. In place of the transmitter, a small remote-controlled bomb was planted in her body, capable of utterly destroying her. The control of the bomb would be in the hands of Tresa Clunard; at the slightest sign of treachery, the Puritan woman would be authorized to detonate the bomb and end Lady A's life once and for all. This, the Head hoped, would give the Empire some insurance against Lady A's betrayal.

When that surgery was accomplished, Lady A was finally permitted to meet the rest of the team that would make the assault with her. The meeting was far from harmonious.

Clunard looked her up and down with evident distaste. "They tell me you're the one responsible for having the FitzHugh robot spying on me," she said.

"I administered the program," Lady A admitted without flinching, "but the idea was originally the PCC's."

"They also tell me you're a robot yourself."

"There are far more blessings to be gained from machines than are dreamed of in your narrow little philosophy. Your whole planet was settled because humanity has the ability to cross interstellar space and live on alien worlds. You can *choose* to live your life of Puritan squalor because machine technology gave you that option. People didn't consider your idea of a 'simple life' so wonderful when it was all they had available to them. You should consider that before you become so preachy."

Despite the animosity on the team, plans went forward for the attack on the PCC's position. At any other time, the Head and his naval counterpart, Lord Admiral

Cesare Benevenuto, would have thrown hundreds of ships into the conflict, supplying enough firepower to destroy all the battle stations and the PCC's asteroid along with them. But circumstances had impoverished them, and an armada of ships could not be spared. Every ship at the planetary bases was needed precisely where it was to guard against rebel attack. Taking a great gamble, Benevenuto assigned thirty ships from Earth's own defensive array, leaving the mother planet dangerously underprotected. The major hopes of the Empire would ride on this mission. If it succeeded, it would provide a knockout punch to the rebellion's forces; if it failed, the Empire might never recover its former glory.

The expeditionary force arrived at the coordinates Lady A had given them, not knowing precisely what to expect. Even assuming their enemy had been telling the truth—which was not by any means a foregone conclusion—the PCC's plans might have been changed without her knowing them. They could have arrived at the designated site and found nothing but empty space, at which point they could only return to Earth and begin again.

But the information they'd gotten was accurate. Facing the small fleet was a double globe of automated battle stations. The battle stations were heavy, lumbering vessels, not capable of any great flight; their sole function was defense, and they would perform that admirably. And right in the center of the concentric globes of defense, safe and secure from the force the Empire brought against it, was the asteroid that housed the Primary Computer Complex.

The Imperial fleet formed itself into a third globe surrounding the other two. With only thirty ships in the formation they were hopelessly spread out through space; Benevenuto would have needed ten times that number to comprise an effective task force. But then, the Navy's role was not to smash the PCC itself, but to provide a diversion while the real assault team slipped through a hole in the computer's defenses.

164

The automated stations watched alertly as the Imperial ships scattered over the surface of their imaginary sphere, just outside of firing range. The battle lines were drawn and the antagonists waited patiently for the order to begin fighting.

At a signal from the flagship, the imperial fleet began converging on the battle stations, their searing rays blazing forth at the enemy. The Navy gunners were aided by the unusual fact that their targets, for once, were perfectly stationary. The disadvantage was that the battle stations' shields were so strong they could withstand almost anything the attack ships could throw at them, and still have plenty of offensive power to hurl back deadly beams against their foes. Two or three of the imperial ships acting together might have been able to overpower the shields of a single battle station and destroy it—but each ship was on its own against the firepower of those deadly stations.

The Navy ships dodged and darted as they made their approach to the globes, but the large battle stations —their surfaces bristling with offensive weaponry— kept them in sight with computer accuracy. Beam after beam scored the flanks of the imperial vessels. Their shields held for a long time, but they were not perfect and they could not withstand indefinitely the fury being flung at them by the rebel stations. As their shields failed, the imperial craft raced out of the conflict to avoid being totally destroyed by enemy fire. It was prudence, rather than cowardice, that dictated this action, as the Empire was already short of fighting ships and could not afford to lose any more.

While all this was going on, one imperial ship held back from the fighting and released a squadron of tiny metallic slivers, moving toward the center of the rebel formation so slowly that they were barely detectable on the sensors. The battle stations' defensive screens would have blocked them out if they were simply torpedos— but they went nowhere near the battle stations, and the automated defenses paid them no attention.

The tiny slivers slipped through the double globe formation as though it weren't there, aiming for the PCC asteroid. The PCC's own defenses sprang to life—but as Lady A had accurately calculated, by the time the small vessels were within range of the asteroid they had reached a blind spot in the defenses. The computer could not see anything so tiny there nor fire accurately at them, and the slivers reached their target safely.

As each tiny space needle crashed into the face of the asteroid, it burst open and a spacesuited figure emerged. The Puritan assault team rallied around Lady A and followed her to a spot in darkest shadow along the rocky surface. The lights of their helmets, shining deep into a fissure, revealed a small airlock hatch, sealed shut for perhaps five decades. The team did not bother trying to open the hatch the normal way; they simply dropped a grenade and blew it open, allowing them access to the inner recesses of the PCC.

As Lady A started inside, the Puritans gathered around the entrance and began their prayers, willing the miraculous powers into their bodies. When they felt infused with the divine force, they got down on hands and knees and crawled through the opening. In this position they couldn't be surprised by sudden changes in the gravitational field.

They were barely inside the corridor when the ultra-grav was switched on, turning the simple hallway into a corridor of agony. Even Lady A's super-strong robot body had trouble moving in this field. She was on all fours like the rest of the team, creeping forward just as slowly as everyone else. Behind her, Tresa Clunard pushed the bomb along the ground as she crawled painfully along the designated route.

The bomb had been carefully designed for this particular mission. It had to be lightweight, since in twenty-five gees even a balloon was a major encumbrance. At the same time it had to carry as much explosive power as possible, since SOTE would not have another chance at this mission; this one bomb would have to demolish a substantial portion of the computer to knock the enemy leader out of action. The mission planners had finally agreed on using a miniaturized nuclear warhead. The explosion itself would physically destroy perhaps a third of the computer's interior—but the electromagnetic pulse that would accompany the nuclear blast would wipe out virtually all electrical activity within the brain. The PCC would cease to exist.

The corridor was in darkness; all the team could see of their surroundings was what showed in the spotlights of their spacesuit helmets. Bare metal floor and walls encompassed their universe.

The optimum point, Lady A informed them, was nearly a hundred meters down the hallway, the full length of a football field. While that was not very far considering the asteroid had a diameter of twenty-five kilometers, it was far enough for a nuclear blast to do the desired damage.

This distance was traversed a centimeter at a time as the group laboriously pulled its way forward across the smooth floor. They did not have to worry about gas, stunners, or blasters; as Lady A had predicted, there were no defenses along this overlooked passageway into the depths of the computer's brain. All the group had to overcome was the ever-present, oppressive gravity that pulled at them and tested every fiber of their being.

Lady A could feel no pain, but for the first time since leaving her flesh-and-blood body behind she knew what it was like to struggle physically against a force greater than herself. The Puritans, even with the power of their faith, were also struggling, and the sounds of their prayers grew louder over their spacesuit radios.

Centimeter by centimeter they crawled forward into the darkness, and the journey seemed to take an eternity. The strain was evident on all their faces as they battled the crushing gravitational force. But slowly, steadily, they crept along until at last they reached the desired point.

Tresa Clunard placed the bomb against the wall. She set the timer as she'd been instructed—but Lady A was watching her and suddenly protested.

"You only set that for a couple of minutes. That doesn't give us enough time to get out of here," she said.

Tresa Clunard looked at her with an other-worldly smile. "The others and I took a vote. We're not leaving. We're going to die here in God's glory, serving His divine mission."

"But I don't believe in your stupid religion."

"You will die as you deserve, here in the belly of your evil master," Clunard said with smug simplicity.

"You're mad," Lady A exclaimed. Fighting the heavy gravity she staggered forward, trying to reach the timer controls on the bomb and reset it. Clunard, seeing this, pressed the button on the special detonator she had.

The small explosive charge planted in Lady A's body went off, ripping the artificial flesh and sending fragments of the Galaxy's most notorious woman flying in all directions. Thus did her dreams of galactic domination end in one explosive moment, and the supposedly immortal Aimée Amorat became little more than a twisted mass of metal and plastiderm.

Tresa Clunard turned to the other Puritans. Her face was calm, accepting. "My friends," she said warmly, "let's sing the praises of God and die with His name on our lips."

Being buried beneath the surface of the asteroid, the nuclear explosion was not visible from the outside—but the electromagnetic radiation generated by the blast easily registered on the Navy's sensor screens. The instant it was detected they disengaged from the combat and backed away out of range of the stations' fire. A subcom message was beamed back to Earth, telling of the mission's success.

The battle stations, being independently automated, did not stop functioning with the destruction of the PCC. They remained positioned in space around the dead hulk of their creator, ready to defend it from any external danger. They still represented a minor hazard to interstellar traffic, and the Navy would eventually send a large fleet of ships in to do a proper job of destroying them. But such a task could wait for a more convenient moment. There was no longer any hurry.

CHAPTER 15

A New Empire

The rebellion did not collapse with the demise of its leader; the PCC had planned too well and organized too efficiently for that. Rebel leaders on many worlds had solidified their positions during the computer's direction of hostilities, and the Imperial forces—still recovering from the devastating blow they'd been dealt—were insufficiently equipped to dislodge them immediately.

But the unity and the superb coordination of rebel efforts that had been the hallmark of the revolution were now gone. There was no single leader with an overall vision to direct the uprising. Insurrectionists on one world no longer had instantaneous knowledge of events on other planets. Supplies could no longer be routed instantly to the places they were needed. The smartest of the rebel chiefs, realizing how important such coordination was, devised their own impromptu communications networks—but they were never as effective as when under PCC direction.

Slowly and unsteadily, at first, the Empire began taking back the planets it had lost. Both sides now had an equal disadvantage with lack of computer coordination.

The difference was that the Imperial forces were better trained than their opponents and had a cause to fight for, whereas the revolutionary armies were mostly mercenaries looking solely for personal profit. The rebel leaders had been chosen more for their organizational abilities than for their knowledge of military tactics, and in the campaign to hold what they'd taken they eventually made mistakes on which the Empire's strategists could capitalize.

Working with its limited resources, the Empire would take seven years to clear away the last vestiges of the revolt and regain total control of the occupied planets once again. During that time, many people would suffer, many would fight, and altogether too many would die to preserve the idea of a unified human government throughout all of space. There would be many tales of personal courage and honor, and—as might be expected—d'Alemberts would figure in more than a few of them. But by the end of that seven years the Empire would have regained its strength and become as strong as ever—and even stronger, in fact, since it would not be nurturing a mechanical traitor in its very core.

But those were all considerations for the future in the days following the destruction of the PCC, and no one then could tell for certain how things would turn out. This was a time for plans and policymaking, and the highest-level thinkers on Earth were working overtime to salvage the concept of Empire. The military strategists were plotting campaigns to recover the lost worlds, and reprogramming the military computers at Luna Base to aid their studies. But by far the most serious planning was being done in the realm of the social sciences. The whole fabric of society had been ripped apart beyond mending; it would have to be rewoven from new threads, trying to maintain as much of the old pattern as possible.

Virtually all vital records had been erased from data banks around the Galaxy. There was no identification, no way of knowing when a person had been born, what grades he'd gotten in school, what his fingerprint and retinal patterns were, whether he'd ever been married and to whom, whether he'd ever had a criminal record, or what his medical history was. With the exception of well-known public figures, a person could be anyone he claimed to be—and while most people naturally stayed within their old social circles and had friends who could vouch for them, there were not a few who took advantage of the chaos to create new identities for themselves. It was a time of rebirth, and out of the ashes rose new opportunities for people to change their lives.

With all the financial records gone, human commerce came to a sudden halt. The Empress's crash program in socialism provided life's basic necessities for most people, but it could not be a long-term solution. Already black markets were springing up in nonessential items, despite the harsh imperial laws against profiteering. People could not be allowed to sit idle for long periods of time, or unrest would naturally result. Riots on top of rebellion could not easily be handled, and alternatives had to be found.

There was no way of telling whether the average person had been a billionaire or a bum, and so eveyone would have to start out equally. Even the nobility, who could at least establish their own identity, could not claim more wealth than their family manors and the personal property they had had on hand at the time of the computer crash—and most of that, by edict, was now state property.

The first priority was to establish a medium of exchange. All the old coins and notes were declared invalid to prevent thievery, swindling, and speculation. The government asked people to turn in their coins for the metal content, although many collectors held on to them, knowing their value would skyrocket in future years.

The old rubles were replaced by units called "imperia." The imperium was based, not on a standard of precious metals as had been done in the past, but on a standard of energy units that more fully reflected the actual cost of goods and services. Each duke was authorized to distribute temporary scrip until new bills could be printed and new coins minted. Financial computers were hurriedly reprogrammed to deal in the new money so credit transactions could take place. It was taken for granted that there would be a lot of counterfeiting at the beginning of the program—and that, too, was made a capital offense. The counterfeiting would taper off as the money was more in circulation and people grew more familiar with it.

The next step was to get people back to work, to start society functioning again. Of highest priority were people in essential services—police, firefighters, and medical workers. In most cases, workers in such fields knew several other people who could vouch for them, so only qualified people were placed in these vital positions. If a person claimed to be trained in one of those jobs—say as a doctor—but had no verifiable references, review boards were established to test the applicant's proficiency in the field. This system assured at least a minimum level of services during the awkward transition phase.

Most people simply returned to the jobs they'd had before the disruption occurred. Coworkers in various shops knew one another and the relationship patterns quickly re-established themselves. If someone tried to take unfair advantage of the situation, perhaps by claiming a higher job than he'd really had, his colleagues would usually band together and denounce him to the authorities. In those instances where a person's position couldn't be verified, the ultimate test was whether he could perform the job; if he could, he was kept on regardless of what he'd done before.

Perhaps the hardest hit of all were not the poor, but the wealthier classes. Since all property had been seized by the government during the crisis, if these people didn't have marketable skills they found themselves without means of gainful employment. Some became office managers, while many others had to apply for job retraining at government expense, and lived off the dole as they did so. These people were probably the bitterest about the turn of fate they'd suffered, and stories were handed down for generations about the fortunes their families had lost in the revolution.

Without a free market economy to set standards, local officials were directed to set up wage and price councils. Each job was carefully evaluated and wages were established for the workers. More bitter fights broke out over this issue than over any other, but such restraints were a necessary evil until society could recover from the blow it had been dealt. Prices were similarly structured to allow wage-earners to afford the necessities of life. Once the wage and price guidelines were in effect, the free food distribution system was ended and people returned to buying what they needed with the money they'd earned from their own labors.

The Empress knew that these measures would not work on a long-term basis, and so a Transitionary Council was appointed to help society work toward the return of a free market state. Every business that had formerly been private, and every piece of property not required for legitimate government function, had a price established for it. As soon as someone—or a group of people pooling their resources—could pay that price, they could buy that business or property from the government. They were then free to do anything with it they liked, subject to the normal laws of commercial practice—but they now had to pay the employees' wages, set their own prices, and pay taxes on their profits. The prospect of becoming a landowner or shareholder in a company provided a tremendous incentive, and most people worked hard to achieve these goals. While many fortunes were lost in the revolution, even more were made. There was no limit to what a person could achieve if he worked hard enough for it. There were bound to be injustices, but in general people were satisfied with the way things turned out.

Economic recovery, too, took longer than many had hoped. It would be a dozen years from the outbreak of the revolution before the Empire had completely returned to a free market economy—but by that time the health of the Empire would once more be assured and people would once again have confidence in their way of life.

One thing that could never be restored, though, was the art lost in the initial catastrophe. The Imperial palaces had been repositories for some of the finest murals, frescoes, paintings, sculpture, and hand-crafted jewelry the Galaxy had ever seen. All that now lay in ruins, with only photographs to remind posterity of what once had been. Most of these treasures had been the personal property of the imperial family, and Edna Stanley grieved for their loss. If any act attested to the heartless, inhuman nature of the enemy, it was this senseless destruction of human beauty.

Ten days after the destruction of the PCC, Empress Stanley Eleven gave a very private dinner party for an elite group of people. Since all the royal palaces had been destroyed and were not yet rebuilt, the Empress commandeered the restaurant of one of Moscow's finest hotels for her private entertainment. The guest list—small for a royal affair—included the Emperor-Consort, Grand Duke Zander von Wilmenhorst, his daughter Helena and her fiancé Captain Paul Fortier, Duke Etienne d'Alembert, Jules and Yvonne d'Alembert, and Pias and Yvette Bavol. As the Empress told them before the meal began, "We were all privy to some of the most decisive moments in the history of the old Empire. I think it's only right that we be here together to oversee the birth of the new Empire."

During the meal the conversation was light. Edna spent most of her time listening as her devoted subjects explained what they'd been doing in the past few weeks to help preserve order within the Galaxy. The Head and his daughter had been reorganizing the entire Headquarters of SOTE on Earth, and Paul Fortier was almost singlehandedly responsible for coordination between SOTE and the Navy. Etienne d'Alembert had been coordinating the reports coming in from the teams he'd sent to rebel-occupied planets, while the two teams of super-agents had been transcribing as many details as they could remember of their adventures for the Service during the hectic years of their careers. The d'Alemberts were a bit reluctant to speak of their family in front of Fortier; even though he'd proven his abilities and loyalties on numerous occasions, they were used to maintaining the strictest secrecy with regard to their family. Only the fact that he was engaged to Helena and obviously destined for a high-level position in Intelligence made them feel safe enough to trust him with such ultra-top-secret information.

"You know, I thought I'd feel relieved when we finally smashed the conspiracy," Yvette said toward the end of the meal. "Instead, I just feel a sort of hollow place inside me. We worked and fought and sweated for years, and then *bang!*, it's over. One quick action and the enemy's all gone. I hardly even had time to draw a breath or cross my fingers."

"I know what you mean," Helena said. "It's like the ringing in your ears when a loud noise stops abruptly."

"We're far from being out of danger," the Head reminded them. "There's still an enormous amount of work to do before any of us can sleep soundly."

Edna Stanley leaned forward and smiled. "I'm glad you brought that subject up; it's really why I invited you all here. I was very serious at the start of the meal about overseeing the birth of a new Empire, because that's what we're doing. The old one is gone; it can never be recaptured, and if we tried to form the new one in exactly the same mold we'd be doomed to failure."

She turned to her husband. "Liu, how did you put it? I remember you expressed it so well."

The Emperor-Consort smiled—a warm, comforting smile. "The Empire of Earth must be like the Earth itself. Hurricanes may blow across the Earth, fire may char it, floods may cover it, but in the end the Earth itself remains. New plants and animals appear where the old ones died, and they are never quite the same, but always the Earth goes on.

"And so it must be with the Empire. People may come and go, institutions may rise and fall, a revolution

175

may sweep away everything before it like a typhoon—but the Empire must remain the bedrock of human existence. If Humanity is to survive in the Galaxy it needs one underlying truth on which to base itself—and that truth will be the Empire. The form of the Empire may change, but the Empire itself will go on. It would be thus even if the computer had won, and we must ensure that the concept of Empire does not die."

"Hear, hear," Duke Etienne murmured softly.

"What we have to do," Edna picked up, "is to see that the new Empire shapes itself along just and fair lines. We reject the concept of machine-like perfection and regimentation, but that doesn't mean we should swing in the other direction. My advisors are coming out with a series of programs designed to promote economic recovery, and I think they'll work—but it will take years before the Empire is healthy again. The revolution has stopped its expansion; with the PCC out of the picture they seem to be concentrating just on holding what they've taken, so there's a good chance we can win it back in time.

"My chief concern, and the real reason I wanted to talk with you all tonight, is the governing of this new Empire. An empress can be only as effective as her means of carrying out her orders; I can pass all the edicts I want, but if they're not enforced they become meaningless. Whatever Empire emerges from these ruins, it will have to administer all the planets as efficiently as did the old one."

She paused and looked around the table. "Whether we like to admit it or not, we're deeply indebted to the PCC for enabling our old Empire to grow. Before the PCC was put into service there were just under nine hundred planets in the Empire and the government was growing a little threadbare, which was why so much money was spent on a computer so large. In the years since, we've expanded by more than fifty percent. I honestly don't believe our Empire could have grown to the size it did without the PCC. Even though it was simultaneously undermining the government, the computer kept it running so efficiently we didn't even notice the sabotage.

"Now we find ourselves in a very awkward position. We're without the services of our primary tool at precisely the moment when we need strong administration the most. The rebels are holding between half and two-thirds of our planets, so for the moment we're relieved of the responsibility for governing them—but the planets we do control need our help desperately. We have to know what their problems are and be able to enforce our solutions quickly, efficiently, and humanely, or we'll risk even more rebellions."

As she glanced around the table her gaze was on the face of every security agent in turn. "We obviously can't repeat our mistake and just build another super-computer that could betray us again under similar conditions. Since we don't know how the PCC became self-aware, we wouldn't know how to prevent it happening in another computer of the same capacity. I'm told the cyberneticists are excited about the concept of artificial intelligence and hope to create another one deliberately—and this time we'll make sure it stays friendly.

"But that won't help us run the Galaxy in the meantime. If we can't rely on our computers, we'll have to put more dependence on the human side. To my way of thinking, this will mean an even larger and more demanding role for the Service of the Empire. This discussion is about the future of you all, as well as of the Empire itself. I'd appreciate your comments."

There was a long awkward silence. Jules cleared his throat and said, "Of course, you know we'll do everything we can."

"I've never doubted that," Edna nodded. "I'm talking about policy and direction. What job should SOTE be doing, and how can we help it work most effectively?"

"I don't think SOTE can, or should, do the whole job," the Head spoke up. As the others looked surprised, von Wilmenhorst elaborated. "Except for the regrettable period under 'Mad Stephanie,' the Service of

177

the Empire has never been, and was never intended to be, a secret police force. Our stated purpose is to keep the Empire running smoothly, and most of our work has been routine—to keep track of interstellar commerce and travel, to facilitate disputes that arise between different planets, and generally to oil the wheels of the galactic machinery. Tracking down traitors has always been important, but it consumed a relatively small percentage of our total manpower—until the PCC–Lady A conspiracy started taking up more and more of our energy. Now that the conspiracy's out in the open, it's the military's job to crush the rebellion and the Service can return to the business of administration.''

"What exactly are you suggesting?'' Edna asked.

"Because of the enormity of the task, and because we won't have the computer coordinating facilities to centralize everything, no one agency can do the whole job. I'd recommend the formation of at least three different organizations to handle the load. The Service of the Empire should return to the task of routine administration. There should be a small but elite internal security agency separate from, but in close contact with, the Service; I think this agency could readily combine the investigative duties of both SOTE and Naval Intelligence, to avoid duplication of effort. Third, there should be a separate department to monitor the workings of the nobility on the local level—again, working closely with the other two organizations.''

"Excuse me, but I don't understand,'' Vonnie interrupted. "Why do we need an organization like that? There's already the Chamber of Thirty-Six and the College of Dukes to do that sort of thing.''

Zander von Wilmenhorst shook his head. "They both deal largely with ceremonial matters. I'm speaking of a more practical organization. Remember, the Empire will have less coordinated access to information from its outlying areas; it will *have* to rely, more than ever, on the grand dukes, dukes, and other local nobility to see that things run properly. Ideally, every noble should be appointed by the current ruler to insure that only the best people are in charge at local levels—but that would mean overturning the Stanley Doctrine of inheritance, and we'd have an immediate revolt from the rest of the Galaxy as well. There'll be a lot of new titles to appoint when this whole mess is over, and we'll have to choose the best possible people—but we can't guarantee how good their heirs will be.

"Because we'll have to rely more on the local nobility, they'll have that much more power—and they'll know it. We'll also have to let them know there's an organization watching them to make sure they don't step too far out of line. SOTE and the new internal security agency will have their hands full with other matters, so I think a separate department should devote itself exclusively to the nobility."

"I'm not sure the division of powers is a good idea," Duke Etienne said. "All three will overlap much of the time. The new SOTE that you described may uncover some erratic behavior on the part of some grand duke, or some earl's misbehavior may mask the beginnings of treason. We're already worried about a lack of coordination; splitting the enforcement between three separate groups only makes the problem worse, not better."

"I agree there'll be a lot of interrelation between the three departments, a lot of room for overlap," von Wilmenhorst nodded. "We don't want to allow interservice rivalries to grow, as they did until recently between SOTE and NI. We'll have to make sure all three branches get along well together and share information smoothly when it becomes necessary. They'll need leaders who work smoothly together—and probably should all be overseen by a single coordinator who can settle any jurisdictional disputes."

He turned to face the Empress. "This is considered an informal meeting, isn't it?"

"Of course," Edna told him.

"Then I can feel a little freer about making specific recommendations, knowing that they're always subject to Your Majesty's best judgment. I have some choices I personally feel would be good for these different departments. I would volunteer, quite immodestly, to be the overall coordinator. Helena has kept SOTE running so smoothly as my assistant that I feel perfectly confident in turning the reins of SOTE over to her. Though it pains my father's heart to admit it, she's not as good a strategist as I am—but the position as I've redefined it calls more for an administrator, which she does far better than I ever could.

"For the internal security agency, I think our Captain Fortier would make an ideal choice. The Admiralty is bound to object if we take the Office of Naval Intelligence away from them, but if the administrator of the security department is a Navy man I think they'll go along. The fact that Paul is marrying Helena means the two departments should be able to work closely together —and if the liaison work they did between SOTE and NI is any indication, the two departments will mesh superbly. We can't always guarantee that the heads of these two departments will be married to one another, but at least we'll start out with close cooperation; we can hope that sets a standard for future behavior."

Helena and Fortier were both blushing; the Grand Duke smiled and turned his attention elsewhere around the table. "As for overseeing the local nobility, I can't think of anyone better qualified than Duke Etienne. As a well-respected duke himself, no one could object to his getting the position—and he's already proved he can administer. He's kept the Circus going all these years. . . ."

"That's just the point," Etienne sputtered in protest. "You're talking about a full-time job. I couldn't do that and manage the Circus, too."

The Grand Duke smiled. "I know I'm sticking my nose in where it doesn't belong, and that the d'Alemberts have always run the Circus in their own way—but it occurs to me that since Jules's recent leg injury will keep him away from the more strenuous undercover assignments in the future, he might be willing to accept a slightly more sedentary position. The Circus will be on hiatus for a while until we recall the teams we sent out;

180

don't you think Jules and Yvonne will be able to manage it well once it's re-formed?''

Duke Etienne was caught in a dilemma set up by his wily friend. He was proud of the work he'd done as Manager of the Circus, and he enjoyed it more than anything he could do in his life. But he was also extremely proud of his son's abilities and of all he'd managed to do in the Galaxy so far. He couldn't very well deny that Jules would run the Circus in an excellent fashion.

"Perhaps," he admitted grudgingly. "But you can't expect an old star rover like me to settle down behind a desk, can you?"

"Nobody said anything about settling down behind a desk," von Wilmenhorst soothed. "If you're going to ride herd on thirty-six grand dukes, hundreds of dukes, and who knows how many thousands of lesser nobles, you'll have to be on the move a lot—more even than you were with the Circus."

"We'll see," Duke Etienne muttered, but Jules caught his eye and made him smile despite himself. Jules looked back at the Head and gave a brief nod, signifying that he would take the position and convince his father—if that was what the Empress wanted.

"You seem to have mapped out a future for everyone but Pias and me," Yvette said. "Where are we going to end up in your plans?"

"You've got your own future mapped out already," von Wilmenhorst told her. "Pias is going to be the next Duke of Newforest, and you'll be his duchess. From all reports, that will be happening in the near future. I'm sorry, Pias, for your father's unfortunate illness, but I'm glad you've reconciled. You and Yvette should return there and spend as much time with him as you can before the end—and also help make a smooth transition to your own administration."

"I'm going to feel so useless," Yvette said. "Everyone else is getting exciting jobs, while Pias and I get to nursemaid a planet. I was always glad Robert was older than I was, so he'd inherit Papa's title and I could do the real work."

"Oh, even as a duke I saw my share of action," her father said with a wink.

"Precisely," von Wilmenhorst added. "As I told you before, there's going to be a lot more responsibility placed on the shoulders of the nobility under the new regime, and you'll be doing important work in holding the Empire together. Besides, I think Newforest represents an underused resource. We've recruited a lot of DesPlainians into the Service, but not many Newforesters; the new internal security agency will need all the good people it can get. You may end up doing some recruiting and training for us. Don't worry—I have a feeling you won't feel slighted at all."

He looked back at the Empress. "Well, you *did* ask for comments, Your Majesty. I know I've talked a lot and been rather free with my assumptions. I'll give you more detailed and formal proposals in writing within a week or so, as soon as my workload permits."

"You've at least given me a lot to think about," Edna told him. "And, as usual, what you say makes a great deal of sense. I knew there would have to be some major shakeups in the organization—it may well be along the lines you suggest.

"In the meantime," she continued, raising her glass, "I'd like to thank all of you for the help you've given me through the years. I can't think of a better way than with the official Service salute: Here's to tomorrow, fellows and friends. May we all live to see it!"

They drank the toast and glasses were refilled. At the end of the table, Jules stood up hesitantly. "Your Majesty, I've been thinking. We've been talking a lot tonight about what's going to happen. At the risk of seeming heretical, I'd like to propose a new official toast."

He raised his glass once again. Up and down the table his dinner companions raised their own glasses and looked at him expectantly as he said, "Here's to tomorrow, fellows and friends. May we make it what we wish it!"

APPENDIX

The Stanley Dynasty

STANLEY ONE: Born George Stanley, 2175. Became King Stanley Six of Earth in 2205, at age 30. Crowned himself Emperor Stanley One of the Empire of Earth in 2215, at age 40. Reigned 31 years—10 as king, 21 as Emperor. Strong and able, but harsh and frequently unjust. Married in 2201, at age 26. Two children: Crown Prince Theobold and Princess Theodora. Assassinated in 2236 at age 61 by his son.

STANLEY TWO: Born Theobold, 2202. Crowned 2236 at age 34 after killing his father. Reigned one year. A bachelor with a harem of concubines; no legitimate offspring. Not content with murdering his father and mother, he tried in 2237 to murder his sister Theodora. The plot backfired and she killed him.

STANLEY THREE: Born Theodora, 2204. Crowned 2237 at age 33 after killing her brother. Reigned 37 years. Married 2233 at age 29. Had 3 children including Crown Prince Karl. First of the Great Stanleys. Consolidated the Empire and founded the Service of the Empire. Established the structure of nobility by elevating selected commoners to noble rank. Propounded the

Stanley Doctrine: strict primogeniture with no distinction as to gender; royalty must and nobility may marry commoners; spouse is elevated to the level of the higher-ranking spouse, except that in any difference of opinion, the decision of the higher-born is final; inbreeding within one-thirty-second consanguinity positively forbidden; full loyalty to the throne is mandatory, with the penalty for failure being death. Stanley Three abdicated at age 70 in 2274 in favor of her oldest son.

STANLEY FOUR: Born Karl, 2235. Crowned 2274 at age 39. Reigned 19 years. Married 2256 at age 21. Had four children: Crown Princess Stephanie, Prince Edmund, Prince Charles, and Princess Charlene. A good ruler, but not great. Assassinated in 2293 at age 58 in a full-scale revolution led by Prince Edmund and Grand Duke Gaspard of Sector Nineteen. This was the first real test of the Navy's tradition of loyalty to the throne and to the Stanley Doctrine. Crown Princess Stephanie was hustled aboard the flagship and kept in Fleet Admiral Simms's own cabin until the rebellion was put down. 728 Navy officers were court-martialed and shot; the rebellion was helpless without the Navy they thought they'd subverted. After a few weeks of turmoil, Stephanie succeeded her father.

STANLEY FIVE: Born Stephanie, 2257. Crowned 2293 at age 36. Reigned six years. Married 2279, age 22. Had five children, the youngest of whom, Prince Edward, was born in 2284. Her first imperial act was to execute the leaders of the rebellion, including her brother Edmund. Because of her frightening experience, she was constantly on the lookout for plots against her, executing hundreds of people and banishing many others to the new, raw planet Gastonia at the far edge of Sector Twenty. She became known as "Mad Stephanie," and her harsh rule inspired many new plots. She, her husband, and four of their five children were assassinated simultaneously in 2299; Prince Edward, then an ensign in the Navy, escaped death only because the plotters did not know and could not find out that Fleet Admiral Simms was guarding him as no one had ever before been guarded. Simms declared martial law and executed not only every person whose guilt was probable—including Prince Charles and Princess Charlene—but also the entire families of everyone convicted, the bloodiest purge in all history. Simms declared himself Regent for the new, underage Emperor.

STANLEY SIX: Born Edward, 2284. Crowned 2299, at age 15. Reigned 42 years—6 under Regent Simms (who, much to everyone's surprise, relinquished the Regency on the day Stanley Six became 21) and 36 on his own. Married in 2312, at age 28; had one child, Crown Princess Evelyn. Considered the second of the Great Stanleys. Advanced the Empire tremendously, strengthened SOTE, promoted the arts and sciences. Fleet Admiral Simms (Ret., but still Head of SOTE) died 2341 at age 94—supposedly of a stroke. (Assassination was later suspected, but not at the time.) Later in the same year, Stanley Six was assassinated by a palace clique who wanted Crown Princess Evelyn as Empress.

STANLEY SEVEN: Born Evelyn, 2313. Crowned 2341 at age 28. Reigned nine years. Official date of her marriage (February 15, 2329) is decidedly questionable, as it was kept secret (and *all* royal marriages are supposed to be imperial functions) until April 8 of that year, and her only child, Crown Prince Rudolph, was born on October 10, 2329, when Evelyn was 16. Considered the weakest Stanley of all—used by cliques of "friends," first one, then another. Was killed in a drunken brawl (2350) by a discarded lover, who also killed her current lover and himself.

STANLEY EIGHT: Born Rudolph, 2329. Crowned 2350 at age 21. Reigned 27 years. Married in 2352 and had three sons, including Crown Prince Ansel. His administration was mediocre; honest, but stodgy and unimaginative. He and his Empress were assassinated, together with the two younger princes and their families, by Crown Prince Ansel in 2377.

STANLEY NINE: Born Ansel, 2353. Crowned 2377 at age 24. Reigned 26 years. Had illegitimate son, Banion, by Aimée Amorat, Duchess of Durward, in

2378; Banion was given Patent of Royalty and title "Prince of Durward." Patent was later revoked upon the birth of legitimate heir, William, born 2379, but Amorat and Banion had disappeared and continued plotting for the throne. Strong but harsh ruler, and able administrator. Inaugurated the Primary Computer Complex, which enabled the Empire to expand tremendously. Killed in 2403 when his personal super-dreadnaught was struck by a derelict vessel immediately after emergence from subspace. Although this is the only such accident on record, SOTE investigators concluded it could not possibly have been prearranged.

STANLEY TEN: Born William, 2379. Crowned 2403 at age 24. Reigned 46 years. Married in 2423 at age 44, very late for a Stanley—deliberately. Also deliberately had only one child, Crown Princess Edna. Third of the Great Stanleys, the greatest to date. Among other achievements, he built SOTE up into the finest security organization that civilization has ever seen. Abdicated at age 70 in favor of his daughter.

STANLEY ELEVEN: Born Edna, 2424. Crowned 2449 at age 25. Married in 2448 at age 24. Survived the Coronation Day Incursion and the insurrection, led by the Primary Computer Complex, which nearly destroyed the Empire. Supervised the rebuilding program that restored the Empire to its former greatness.